MW01205669

Contents

Prologue

In the quiet town of Snowy Oaks, Vermont, middle school was an unforgiving battleground. Between science fairs and cafeteria pizza Fridays, reputations were built, broken, and cemented for life. And for Melanie Jenkins, her defining moment came during eighth grade math class.

It started like any other miserable Tuesday. The room buzzed with the chaos of middle schoolers who hadn't yet mastered the concept of "indoor voices." Melanie sat at her desk, scribbling in the margins of her notebook. Doodles of geometric hearts and uneven stars trailed alongside equations she didn't care much about.

"Hey, Moose."

The voice came from behind her. Brent Miltmore.

Melanie stiffened. She hated that nickname. It had started last year, thanks to an unfortunate Halloween costume involving cardboard antlers. Brent had latched onto it like a leech and hadn't let go.

"Leave me alone, Brent," she said without turning around.

"Oh, come on," he said, sliding into the desk behind hers. "Don't be so sensitive. You know it's just a joke."

Melanie clenched her pencil, willing herself to ignore him. But Brent wasn't done.

"Hey, Moose," he said again, louder this time. "Where'd you leave your antlers? Did the forest ranger take them back?"

A snicker rippled through the class. Melanie felt her face heat up.

"Shut up," she muttered under her breath.

"What was that?" Brent leaned forward, his voice dripping with mock sweetness. "Did you say something, stupid Moose?"

She turned around, her black hair swinging like a curtain. "I said shut up."

"Ooh, scary!" Brent said, holding up his hands in mock fear. "What are you gonna do, charge at me?"

The class erupted into laughter. Melanie's hands balled into fists under the desk.

Mrs. Harper, the math teacher, looked up from her desk with an exasperated sigh. "Brent, quit bothering Melanie and focus on your worksheet."

"Yes, Mrs. Harper," Brent said with exaggerated politeness, but the grin on his face told Melanie he wasn't finished.

And sure enough, ten minutes later, as Mrs. Harper erased equations on the chalkboard, Brent struck again.

"Hey, Melanie," he whispered, leaning closer. "Do moose even know how to do math? Or do you just stomp on the calculator until it gives up?"

That was it. The final straw. Melanie turned around, her face blazing. "I said shut up, Brent!"

"Oh, sorry," he said, smirking. "Did I hurt your feelings, Moose?"

Before she knew what she was doing, Melanie's fist shot out. It wasn't graceful or planned, but it landed squarely on Brent's nose with a satisfying crunch.

The room went dead silent.

Brent let out a howl, clutching his nose as blood dripped onto his desk. "What the—she hit me!"

Melanie stood frozen, her fist still clenched, as if her body couldn't believe what it had just done. Around her, the other kids stared in shock. Then, slowly, the whispers started.

"Did you see that?"

"She just punched him!"

"Brent Miltmore got decked by a girl!"

Mrs. Harper whirled around, chalk falling from her hand. "Melanie Jenkins! What is going on?"

Melanie snapped out of her daze, suddenly hyper-aware of the burning sting in her knuckles. "He started it!" she blurted out, pointing at Brent.

"She broke my nose!" Brent wailed, still clutching his face. "She's crazy!"

Mrs. Harper sighed and pinched the bridge of her nose. "Melanie, go to the principal's office. Now."

"But—"

"Now."

Melanie grabbed her backpack and marched out of the room, her heart pounding. Behind her, she could still hear Brent's exaggerated groans and the whispers of her classmates.

"Sit down, Melanie," Principal Fletcher said, his voice weary as he gestured to the chair across from his desk. Melanie plopped down, crossing her arms.

"I didn't mean to hit him," she said quickly, before he could start. "But he wouldn't stop—he was calling me names and—"

"Melanie." Principal Fletcher held up a hand. "You can't go around punching people, no matter what they say."

"But it's not fair!" Melanie argued. "He's been picking on me for months, and no one does anything about it. What was I supposed to do?"

Principal Fletcher sighed, leaning back in his chair. "Melanie, I understand that Brent can be... difficult. But violence isn't the answer."

Melanie scowled, slouching in her chair. "It worked, didn't it? He's not going to call me Moose anymore."

"Be that as it may," Principal Fletcher said, steepling his fingers, "you're getting detention. Three days. And I'll be calling your parents."

"Great," Melanie muttered under her breath.

By the end of the day, the entire school had heard about "The Great Nose Incident." Brent showed up to the afternoon assembly with gauze stuffed in his nostrils, glaring at anyone who dared look at him. Melanie, meanwhile, spent the rest of the day avoiding eye contact and pretending not to hear the whispers.

When her mom picked her up from school, Melanie braced herself for a lecture. Instead, her mother just sighed. "I hope you learned something from this."

"I learned that Brent Miltmore's nose bleeds a lot," Melanie said.

Her mother sighed again. "Go to your room."

By the time Melanie got home that afternoon, the adrenaline had worn off, leaving her with a sick feeling in her stomach. The moment she opened the front door to her family's modest, slightly cluttered home, she was greeted by the smell of soy sauce and garlic. Her mom, a no-nonsense woman with a penchant for overwatering plants, stood at the kitchen counter chopping green onions with the precision of a surgeon.

"Take your shoes off," her mom said without turning around.

Melanie kicked off her sneakers, her backpack sagging on her shoulder. "Mom, I—"

"I heard," her mom interrupted, her tone deceptively calm.

Melanie winced. Of course her mom had already heard. In a town as small as Snowy Oaks, news traveled faster than a sneeze in flu season.

"Let me explain," Melanie started.

Her mom set the knife down and turned to face her, hands on her hips. "You punched a boy in the face. What's there to explain?"

"He called me a stupid moose!" Melanie blurted out, her voice rising in frustration. "And it wasn't just today—he's been picking on me forever! I just... I lost it."

Her mom's expression softened, but only slightly. "Melanie, I understand he hurt your feelings. But fighting is not the answer.

Now you're the one in trouble."

Melanie threw her backpack onto the couch, flopping down next to it. "It's not fair. Brent never gets in trouble for being a jerk, but I throw one punch and suddenly I'm the bad guy?"

Her mom sighed, walking over to sit beside her. "Sometimes life isn't fair. But you can't let people like Brent Miltmore dictate how you behave. You're better than that."

Melanie stared at her hands, still faintly red from the punch. "I just wanted him to stop."

"I know," her mom said gently, brushing a strand of hair out of Melanie's face. "And I'm proud of you for standing up for yourself. But next time, try using your words instead of your fists, okay?"

Melanie nodded reluctantly. "Okay."

Her mom smiled and patted her knee before standing up. "Now go wash up. Dinner's almost ready."

Across town, in the grand Miltmore estate, Brent Miltmore sat in the plush velvet armchair of his bedroom, scowling at his reflection in the ornate gold-framed mirror. His nose was red and swollen, the gauze stuffed inside making him look ridiculous.

"Melanie Jenkins is a psychopath," he muttered, gingerly touching the bridge of his nose and wincing.

From the doorway, John North, the family's butler, raised an eyebrow. "That psychopath broke your nose because you were being a little brat."

Brent glared at him. "She attacked me for no reason!"

"Uh-huh," John said, crossing his arms. "And I suppose she just imagined you calling her a moose?"

Brent flushed, his indignation faltering. "It was just a joke."

"Some joke," John said dryly. "You've been needling that girl for months. Honestly, I'm surprised she didn't deck you sooner."

Brent fumed, his face turning as red as his nose. "You're supposed to be on my side!"

"I am on your side," John said, his tone patient but firm. "But maybe this is a good time for you to learn that actions have consequences. You can't go around treating people like they're beneath you, Brent. Not everyone's going to put up with it."

Brent crossed his arms, sulking. "She still shouldn't have hit me."

"No, she shouldn't have," John agreed. "But you shouldn't have pushed her to it, either."

For a moment, Brent said nothing, his mind replaying the punch over and over. He remembered the fire in Melanie's eyes, the way she hadn't hesitated for even a second.

"I hate her," he muttered.

John chuckled. "Sure you do, kid. Now, how about we put some ice on that nose before it swells up like a balloon?"

<hr />

By the next morning, "The Great Nose Incident" was all anyone at Snowy Oaks Middle School could talk about. Melanie walked into homeroom with her head held high, determined not to let the whispers and stares get to her.

"There she is," someone whispered as she passed.

"That's the girl who punched Brent Miltmore."

"She's crazy!"

Melanie ignored them, sliding into her seat near the back of the room. She wasn't ashamed of what she'd done—if anything, she was proud. Brent had deserved it, and for once, he'd been put in his place.

But pride didn't make the rest of the day any easier. Teachers gave her wary looks, as if she might snap and punch them too. Her classmates either avoided her altogether or pestered her with questions about the fight.

"Did it hurt?"

"Did he cry?"

"Do you think you'll get suspended?"

"No," Melanie snapped, shoving her books into her locker. "And no, I'm not going to teach you how to punch someone, so stop asking."

She spent lunch hiding in the library, grateful for the quiet. She knew the buzz would die down eventually—it always did—but for now, she just wanted to get through the day without losing her temper again.

Meanwhile, Brent spent the day milking his injury for all it was worth. He showed up to school late, sporting a fresh bandage on his nose and an exaggerated limp that had nothing to do with the punch.

"Poor Brent," one girl cooed as he walked into English class.

"Are you okay?"

"I'll survive," Brent said dramatically, sinking into his seat with a pained expression. "But I might have a scar."

The girls around him gasped, hanging on his every word. Brent basked in the attention, conveniently leaving out the part where he'd provoked Melanie into hitting him.

That evening, Melanie's parents sat in the living room, her mom perched stiffly on the edge of the couch, her dad sprawled in his favorite armchair with a cup of tea in one hand and a half-eaten cookie in the other. The tension between them was thick enough to slice with a butter knife.

"You know, I have to say," Howard Jenkins began, dunking his cookie into the tea, "our daughter has a mean right hook. I mean, really—bam! Brent didn't know what hit him."

"Howard," her mom said sharply, glaring at him. "This isn't a joke."

"I'm not joking," Howard said, holding up his hands in mock surrender. "I'm just saying, maybe we should channel that energy. Boxing lessons, maybe? Muay Thai?"

"Howard," her mom repeated, her tone icy. "This is serious. Melanie punched a boy in the face. At school. In front of everyone."

"Well, in her defense, the boy was being a little punk," Howard said, shrugging. "Calling her a moose? Come on, he had it coming."

"That doesn't make it acceptable," her mom snapped, crossing her arms. "She can't just go around hitting people every time someone says something she doesn't like. We've clearly failed to teach her proper discipline."

"Failed?" Howard leaned forward, eyebrows raised. "Come on, Helen, that's a little dramatic. She's a good kid. She just has a temper. Wonder where she gets that from?" He grinned, earning himself a scathing look.

"This isn't about me," Helen said firmly. "It's about what's best for Melanie. And what's best for her is structure. Stability."

"Structure?" Howard echoed. "What, you want to send her to military school?"

Helen ignored him, her tone softening just slightly. "I've been thinking about this for a while. About what's best for her. For all of us. Maybe it's time for a change."

Howard's grin faded. "What kind of change?"

Helen hesitated, then took a deep breath. "I think we should go to Los Angeles. My sister's been asking us to come for months. Melanie needs to get away from Snowy Oaks. This town is too small. Everyone knows what happened. She'll be 'the girl who punched Brent Miltmore' forever if we stay."

"L.A.?" Howard leaned back in his chair, scratching his chin. "You think that's the answer? Uprooting her life?"

"I think staying here is the worse option," Helen said. "She needs a fresh start. And honestly... so do we."

Howard was quiet for a moment, staring into his tea. Then he sighed, a small, lopsided smile creeping back onto his face. "You're probably right. You're usually right. Drives me nuts, but there it is."

Helen rolled her eyes but couldn't hide her faint smile. "So you'll agree?"

"I'll agree," Howard said, pointing a finger at her, "but only if you admit one thing."

"What?" Helen asked warily.

"That our daughter breaking Brent Miltmore's nose is, hands down, the best thing to happen in this town since the bake sale scandal of '98."

Helen groaned, standing up and grabbing his empty tea cup. "You're impossible."

"And you love me for it," Howard called after her, a twinkle in his eye.

In her bedroom upstairs, Melanie lay awake, staring at the ceiling. She had no idea her life was about to change in ways she couldn't yet imagine.

The next morning, Melanie sat at the kitchen table, still groggy from a restless night. Her dad was humming some tune from the 80s as he flipped pancakes, occasionally flicking batter on the counter. Her mom stood at the sink, meticulously wiping down the already-clean faucet, her version of "subtle" stress management.

"You're up early," her dad said with a grin, sliding a pancake onto her plate.

"Couldn't sleep," Melanie mumbled, poking at the pancake with her fork.

"Well, we've got something to talk about," her mom interjected, turning around and drying her hands on a towel.

Melanie froze, her fork hovering mid-air. "What's wrong?"

"Nothing's wrong," her dad said quickly, though the look her mom shot him suggested he wasn't quite telling the truth.

"Your father and I have been thinking," her mom began, her tone measured, "and we've decided it's time for some changes. For the family."

"What kind of changes?" Melanie asked, narrowing her eyes.

Her dad cleared his throat, leaning against the counter. "We've been talking about moving to Los Angeles. To stay with your Aunty Ah Lam for a while."

Melanie blinked. "What?"

"It's just an idea," her mom said quickly. "But we think it could be good for all of us. A fresh start."

Melanie stared at her parents, trying to process what she was hearing. Los Angeles? She'd never even been on an airplane, let alone considered living in a massive city like L.A.

"You're kidding, right?" she said, looking between them.

"It's not as bad as it sounds," her dad said, his tone light. "Your aunt's got a big place. A pool. You love pools."

Melanie wasn't convinced. "What about school? And my friends?"

Her mom hesitated, and Melanie knew instantly she'd already thought of every excuse she could make. "Melanie, let's be honest.

This town isn't exactly doing you any favors right now. People talk. You don't deserve to be stuck with a reputation because of one incident."

"It wasn't just one incident," her dad added, earning a glare from her mom. "What? I'm just saying!"

Melanie crossed her arms. "So you're punishing me for standing up for myself?"

"No," her mom said firmly. "We're trying to help you. And this isn't just about you, Melanie. Your father and I... we've decided to separate."

The words hit Melanie like a slap. She stared at her mom, feeling like the floor had been ripped out from under her.

"You're separating?" she said, her voice cracking.

Her dad moved closer, his easygoing expression replaced with something softer, sadder. "Honey, your mom and I love you. And we're still a team when it comes to you. But we've realized we're better off living apart."

Melanie's throat tightened. "This is my fault, isn't it? Because of what happened with Brent."

"No!" her parents said in unison.

"This has nothing to do with you," her mom added, her voice gentler than Melanie had heard in a long time. "This is about us. And what's best for all of us right now is a fresh start. I'll take you to Los Angeles, and your dad will come visit. You'll see him all the time."

Melanie looked at her dad, hoping he'd tell her this was all some elaborate prank. But he just nodded, giving her a small, sad smile.

"It'll be okay, kiddo."

Two weeks later, Melanie stood in the driveway of her childhood home, staring at the U-Haul hitched to the back of her mom's SUV. Most of their things were already packed and loaded. The house looked oddly bare, stripped of the small touches that had made it feel like home.

Her dad stood beside her, hands in his pockets. "You ready for your big adventure?" he asked, trying to sound cheerful.

Melanie shrugged. "I guess."

"Hey," he said, nudging her gently. "It's not the end of the world. You'll like L.A. Sun, beaches, celebrities. And Aunty Ah Lam's got cable, which is more than I can say for this place."

Melanie couldn't help but smile. "You hate cable."

"True," he said with a wink. "But you don't. Plus, you'll be back to visit before you know it. And when you do, we can team up and beat your mom at Scrabble."

Melanie laughed, even though her chest still felt heavy. "You always cheat at Scrabble."

"Only because your mom uses words like 'qi' and 'zha.' That's not English!"

She turned to him, suddenly serious. "You promise I'll come back? That this isn't... forever?"

Her dad crouched down so they were eye-level. "I promise. You're not losing me, Mel. No matter where you are, I'll always be your dad. And I'll always be here for you."

A lump formed in her throat, but she nodded. "Okay."

"Good," he said, standing up and ruffling her hair. "Now, go help your mom before she tries to pack the entire kitchen."

Melanie nodded again and headed toward the car, feeling like she was leaving more than just her hometown behind.

❧ ♡ ☙

For the first time in over a decade, the Jenkins household felt eerily quiet. Howard sat on the couch that evening, staring at the empty space where Melanie's shoes used to pile up by the door. He missed her already.

Across town, Brent Miltmore sat in his room, scowling at his unfinished math homework. His nose had healed, but his bruised ego hadn't. Part of him was relieved Melanie Jenkins was gone—no more surprise punches to worry about.

But another part of him—a small, unacknowledged part—wondered what life would be like without her.

❧ ♡ ☙

The plane ride to Los Angeles was the longest three hours of Melanie's life. She sat sandwiched between her mom, who was meticulously reviewing a folder of job applications, and a man snoring loudly into her other ear. She didn't mind flying, but the turbulence in her stomach had nothing to do with the bumpy skies.

When they landed at LAX, the chaos of the airport overwhelmed her senses—bright lights, loud announcements, and the buzz of people moving in every direction. It was nothing like Snowy Oaks, where the loudest thing was the occasional snowplow.

"Stick close," her mom said, gripping Melanie's shoulder as they navigated through the crowd. Her mom's voice was brisk and efficient, like she was already mentally checking off tasks. "Aunty Ah Lam's waiting for us at baggage claim."

Melanie nodded, clutching her backpack like a lifeline. The whole thing felt surreal. A week ago, she'd been sitting in her quiet room in Vermont, listening to the sound of wind through the trees. Now she was in the middle of Los Angeles, where even the air smelled busier.

When they finally reached baggage claim, Aunty Ah Lam was waiting with a wide smile and an even wider floppy hat.

"There you are!" Ah Lam said, pulling Melanie into a hug. "Welcome to sunny California, sweetie!"

Melanie let herself be hugged, though it felt like stepping into an entirely different atmosphere. Ah Lam smelled like perfume and sunscreen, a mix Melanie couldn't associate with anyone else in her life.

"Hi, Aunty Ah Lam," Melanie said softly.

"Hi, nothing!" Ah Lam said, holding her at arm's length to look her over. "You've grown so much! The last time I saw you, you were this tall." She held her hand somewhere around Melanie's waist.

"Thanks," Melanie said awkwardly, glancing at her mom.

Ah Lam turned to Helen with a knowing smile. "You must be exhausted. Don't worry, I've got everything set up at the house. Melanie, you're going to love it. Your room has a balcony!"

Melanie perked up slightly at that. A balcony sounded nice, even if it wouldn't overlook the forests she was used to.

As they loaded their luggage into Ah Lam's SUV and drove through the sprawling city streets, Melanie stared out the window in awe. Los Angeles was nothing like Snowy Oaks. There were palm trees instead of maples, skyscrapers instead of steepled churches, and freeways instead of quiet two-lane roads.

"It's... big," Melanie said finally, earning a chuckle from Ah Lam.

"That's one way to describe it," Ah Lam said. "Don't worry, you'll get used to it. Pretty soon, this will feel like home."

Melanie's new room was as different from her old one as Los Angeles was from Snowy Oaks. Her Aunty Ah Lam had decorated it with bright, cheerful colors—yellow curtains, a floral bedspread, and a soft rug that felt like walking on clouds. True to Ah Lam's word, there was a small balcony overlooking the backyard, where a sparkling pool glistened in the sunlight.

"It's nice," Melanie admitted when her mom came in to check on her later that evening.

Her mom nodded, standing in the doorway with her arms crossed. "I know it's a big adjustment. But I think this will be good for us. For you."

Melanie didn't answer right away. Instead, she walked to the balcony door and slid it open, stepping outside. The air smelled different here—warmer, drier, with a faint hint of chlorine from the pool below.

"I miss Dad," she said quietly.

Her mom's expression softened. "I know you do. And you'll see him soon. He's already planning a trip out here next month."

Melanie nodded, still staring at the backyard. She didn't want to cry, but her throat felt tight.

"We're going to be okay," her mom said, her voice softer now. "This is just the beginning of something new. You'll make friends. You'll find your place."

Melanie wasn't so sure. Snowy Oaks might have been small and stifling at times, but it had been home. This new place felt too big, too loud, too... different.

❦ ♡♡ ❦

A few weeks after the move, Melanie found a letter waiting for her on the kitchen counter. It was addressed to her in messy handwriting she recognized immediately.

Brent Miltmore.

She stared at the envelope for a moment, confused. Why would *he* write to her?

"You gonna open it, or just stare at it?" her aunt teased as she passed by with a glass of iced tea.

Melanie frowned, grabbing the envelope and retreating to her room. She sat cross-legged on the bed, carefully tearing it open.

The letter was short—barely two sentences.

Dear Melanie,

Thanks for breaking my nose. Now I don't have to smell all the cow poop in this stupid town.

Brent

Melanie stared at the note, her confusion giving way to a snort of laughter. Of course Brent would send something like this. Even from hundreds of miles away, he managed to be the same obnoxious jerk.

She stuffed the letter into her nightstand drawer, shaking her head. For the first time since the move, she felt something familiar. Annoyance, sure, but also amusement.

Los Angeles might not feel like home yet, but at least one thing hadn't changed: Brent Miltmore was still a pain in the neck.

Melanie stared at the nightstand drawer where she'd shoved Brent's letter, her lips twitching with a reluctant smile. Even from hundreds of miles away, the boy managed to needle her. How exactly had he found time in his cow-poop-filled schedule to write her a letter, anyway? Wasn't he busy terrorizing some other poor soul back in Snowy Oaks?

She let out a groan and flopped backward onto her bed, staring at the ceiling. She could almost hear his voice in that smarmy, know-it-all tone: *"Thanks for breaking my nose."* Who even *thanked* someone for that?

"I hope he stepped in the cow poop," she muttered, rolling onto her side.

The thing was, despite the irritation, the letter had made her laugh. Not a dainty, sophisticated laugh, but a full-blown snort that echoed through her room like a startled piglet. For the first time since moving to Los Angeles, she didn't feel like a fish flopping out of water. Somehow, the thought of Brent, sitting in his big fancy room with his probably-too-perfect handwriting, carefully crafting a letter about cow poop, made the world feel just a little smaller—and a whole lot funnier.

Melanie sat up in bed, the snort-laugh still reverberating in her chest. "Unbelievable," she muttered, shaking her head. Brent Miltmore had a way of worming his way under her skin even when he was half a country away.

For a split second, she considered writing back. But what could she even say? *"Dear Brent, you're still the most annoying person on Earth. Love, Melanie"?* Nah. Giving him the satisfaction wasn't worth it.

Or was it?

She grabbed a notepad from her desk and started jotting down ideas. The first draft read:

Dear Brent,

Glad to know you're still whining. Also, cow poop isn't as bad as your personality.

She crossed it out. Too harsh.

The second attempt was slightly better:

Dear Brent,

You're welcome. But don't forget, the smell of cow poop suits you perfectly.

She tapped the pen against her chin, contemplating whether to tone it down or double down. Ultimately, she folded the note in half and stuffed it in the nightstand next to Brent's letter.

For now, she'd let him think he'd won. But she wasn't above sending a reply if he dared to write again.

Meanwhile, Back in Snowy Oaks...

In his sprawling bedroom, Brent Miltmore leaned back in his chair, staring at the now-empty envelope he'd sent to Melanie.

"She probably didn't even read it," he grumbled.

"You wrote her a letter?" John North, his ever-patient butler, leaned against the doorframe with a smirk.

"No," Brent lied, far too quickly.

John crossed his arms. "Uh-huh. What'd you say? 'Dear Melanie, sorry for being an insufferable brat?'"

Brent scowled. "Of course not. I thanked her for breaking my nose."

John raised an eyebrow. "You thanked her?"

"It's called strategy," Brent said, spinning his chair toward the window. "She's probably feeling guilty now. Serves her right."

John let out a low whistle. "You're playing a dangerous game, kid. Melanie Jenkins doesn't strike me as the guilty type. She's the... punch-you-in-the-face-and-move-on type."

Brent didn't respond, but deep down, he knew John was right. Melanie wasn't the type to back down, and he wasn't sure why he'd bothered writing her at all. Maybe he just missed the banter, as infuriating as it had been.

Or maybe—and this thought he refused to entertain for more than half a second—he just missed her.

As Melanie lay in bed that night, staring at the faint glow of the moonlight spilling through her window, she thought about Snowy Oaks. About the trees she used to climb, the snowball fights she used to win, and even the smell of the small-town diner that served pancakes all day.

She thought about Brent, too—how his smug grin had made her blood boil, how he always seemed to push her buttons without even trying. And how, despite it all, he'd made her laugh in a way she hadn't laughed since moving to Los Angeles.

"Stupid Brent," she muttered under her breath, but there was no venom in the words.

Tomorrow would be another day of figuring out this strange, sprawling city. She'd get lost in her new school's labyrinth of hallways, stumble over unfamiliar names, and keep dodging questions about her Vermont accent.

But for now, she closed her eyes, clutching the tiniest piece of home—the laughter, the irritation, and the ridiculousness that only Brent Miltmore could provide.

And for the first time in weeks, Melanie felt like she wasn't so far away after all.

Chapter 1

Melanie Jenkins

M elanie Jenkins bounced into the ER exam room, her smile brighter than the flickering lights above. She waved a stack of papers like a victory flag.

"Mr. Finney," she called out cheerfully. "Good news! I have your discharge papers. You are all set to go home."

Gertrude Finney, sitting in a worn-out chair, let out a big sigh of relief. "Oh, thank heavens! We thought Alfred was having a heart attack. I was so scared."

"Nope. Just a case of really bad indigestion." Melanie offered a caring smile. She turned to Alfred, who was looking both confused and relieved on the exam table. She understood what fear and panic was.

Melanie's smile softened as she looked at the couple. Alfred and Gertrude were good people. Both in their late sixties. Retired. Happily married. They still held hands, reminding her of a sweet old love story. "Mr. Finney, all of your blood work came back just fine. The two EKGs we took were absolutely normal."

Alfred Finney listened to Melanie, soaking up her words like a sponge. At thirty-five, she wasn't some rookie nurse still smelling of textbooks and energy drinks. Nope, she had experience.

But there was more to Melanie than just her experience as a nurse that Alfred liked. Melanie wasn't exactly cover girl material. She was more "adorkable" than "drop-dead gorgeous." Her glasses were thick enough to see into next week. Black hair with silly bangs that rolled around the corner of her ears. Rosy pink cheeks that played matchy-matchy with her bubble-gum pink nurse scrubs.

Melanie probably wasn't the girl all the boys chased in high school. More likely, she was the one they asked for help with homework. But that was A-OK in Alfred's book. Because while Melanie might not win any beauty contests, she'd definitely take first prize in kindness. And to Alfred, that was way more important than looking like a movie star.

"I feel better," Alfred said, trying to sound tough.

"Good." Melanie replied with a grin. "Mr. Finney, you have no history of heart trouble. But you do have a tummy problem. Dr. Malone wants you to follow up with your doctor." Melanie gently poked Alfred's tummy. "And lay off the spicy foods until you do."

"Is there anything else we should do, Melanie?" Gertrude chirped as worry lines etched on her forehead.

Melanie met the concerned gaze with a reassuring smile. "Mrs. Finney, I promise you that Mr. Finney's problem is not heart related. All of his tests came back fine. On top of that, you arrived at the ER right when Dr. Grayson was here. Dr. Grayson is the top cardiologist in the state. He went over Mr. Finney's test results and he listened to Mr. Finney's heart on three different occasions. If Dr. Grayson says the old ticker is good, then the old ticker is good."

"I was very scared," Gertrude admitted, clutching her pearls. "I've never seen Alfred grab his chest like that before. Nearly gave me a heart attack of my own!"

Melanie bent low and took Gertrude's hands. "My Dad has bad tummy problems. He thought he was having a heart attack on more than one occasion. That old poop is seventy-five years old and still going strong. His heart is healthier than mine." Melanie smiled. "Maybe because he had me when he was forty. I kept him running all these years."

Tears began falling from Gertrude's eyes. "You're such a blessing. Most nurses are very rude and uncaring."

Melanie grinned and replied, "Well, I'm half Asian, half amazing. It's a potent combo." She tipped Gertrude a wink and then gently wiped her tears away. "Now, let's get Mr. Finney home. You've been here all night, and it's nearly seven. My shift ends in twenty minutes, so I'll be trading my scrubs for pajamas right behind you."

Gertrude hugged Melanie and then signed the discharge papers. She turned to Alfred, wagging a finger. "No more fancy foreign food for you, mister." She jangled the car keys. "I'm driving. Your job is to sit still and not scare me half to death again."

Alfred shot Melanie a playful look. "I think I was better off here," he teased.

Melanie saw Alfred and Gertrude off and then went to check on an old woman named Lilly. Lilly had been brought into the ER by ambulance. An hour later, a half-drunk woman who claimed to be

Lilly's daughter showed up.

"How are you feeling, dear?" Melanie asked as she checked Lilly's IV bag.

"My back's killing me."

"I'm surprised you're still awake. We've given you enough pain meds to knock out a horse." Melanie glanced around the room. "By the way, where's your daughter?"

"I told her to go home," Lilly spoke in a tired voice. She reached out a weak hand and touched Melanie. "I did doze off a few times. I dreamed of you."

"Oh?" Melanie gave Lilly her full attention. The poor soul looked so frail and alone. "I hope you dreamed something good. Did I win the lottery?"

"No." Lilly's sleepy eyes suddenly cleared and became fierce. "I dreamed you were getting married."

"Married?" Melanie chuckled. "Ms. Statesmore, the only aisle I'm walking down is at the grocery store."

"I'm serious. You were getting married. I didn't see to who, though?" Lilly insisted. She squeezed Melanie's hand. "Leave this hospital, child. This hospital is taking too much of your life away."

"Oh, you don't need to preach to the choir. I'm working out my last two weeks as we speak. In fact, this is my very last shift." Melanie smiled into Lily's eyes. "I'm leaving Los Angeles and moving all the way across the country to Vermont."

"Vermont?" Lilly's eyebrows shot up. "Dear me! You're really shaking things up, aren't you? What will you do there?"

"I've accepted a job as a live-in nurse," Melanie explained. "I was born and raised in Vermont. It's going to be nice to get back home. Los Angeles and I never clicked. I moved here after my parents split. Mom went back to Singapore, and Dad stayed in Vermont."

Lilly listened, then nodded. "You're a pretty girl, honey. Your eyes are kind, but they're sad too. Like you're missing something. Go home. Find someone to love before you get old and cranky like me."

With that, Lilly's eyes fluttered shut, and she was out like a light.

"What a sweet woman," Melanie whispered. She tucked Lilly in, checked her vitals, and got ready to leave. "Love refuses to find me... maybe someday. Goodbye, Lilly."

Melanie walked back to the nurses' station. It was finally time to end her last and final shift at a miserable hospital that felt like a prison. "So, this is it, huh, girl?" a nurse named Heather asked.

"My SUV is packed full. I turned in the keys to my apartment last night. I'm leaving this hospital and driving into Nevada. I'm not stopping until I get to Las Vegas."

"After pulling a twelve-hour shift? Girl, you'll be a zombie behind the wheel!"

"The sooner I get to Vermont, the better, Heather." Melanie said, glancing around. Not a single doctor or nurse had come to wish her well—except for Dr. Grayson. Only Dr. Grayson had stopped by earlier. And Heather, of course.

"LA's been good to me, but Vermont's peaceful countryside feels like my next chapter."

Heather looked at Melanie. Yes, Melanie was a tad bit on the dorky side—at least in the looks department. When Melanie was off duty she dressed like a discarded hippie. That was okay. Heather saw Melanie's heart. It was pure gold. Melanie was what Heather called a "Tender Soul."

The only problem was the poor woman couldn't find love if her life depended on it. Heather had set Melanie up on countless dates—and each date ended in disaster. Maybe it was the way Melanie laughed? When Melanie worked up a good laugh she snorted her head off. Or maybe it was her silly bangs or oversized eyeglasses?

"I'm gonna miss you," Heather said.

"You have three teenagers to take care of and a fussy husband. You won't miss me for long." Melanie said, giving Heather a big hug. "But I'll call you. And hey, I'll write and send pics of Vermont's finest... cows farting."

Heather cracked up. "I'll hold you to that!"

Melanie looked at her friend. Even with forty creeping up on her, Heather still looked like she could be on a magazine cover. "You know you're my bestie, right? This isn't goodbye-goodbye."

"I know it isn't." Heather fought back a tear. She loved Melanie to bits, but worried her friend might end up old and alone while watching a bunch of cows farting.

After ending her shift and having a quick meeting with the HR manager, Melanie hurried out into an overcrowded parking garage. Hurried? Run is more like it. She ran to an old Bronco and dived into the passenger seat. "I'm free! I did it! I actually did it!" she shouted. "I've already completed all the requirements to transfer my nursing license to Vermont. I'll start working for Mrs.

Miltmore on October 1st! This is really happening!"

Melanie fumbled for her phone, nearly dropping it in her excitement. She hit speed dial.

"Hey dad, I'm getting ready to leave the hospital now! I should be in Las Vegas in a few hours!"

Howard Jenkins smiled from ear to ear. He couldn't wait to have his daughter home. "I'll be waiting with open arms."

"And lots of gas," Melanie teased.

Howard blushed. Melanie always teased him about his... uh... gas issue. "I take my medication as prescribed."

"Oh dad, you know I'm only teasing," Melanie giggled.

Howard heard cars honking in the background. "Are you on the highway?"

"No, I'm still in the parking garage. It's a nightmare trying to get out of here when shift change happens. I've learned to wait a few minutes and let the eager beavers kill each other before I dive into the water."

"That's my girl. Smart as always," Howard said beaming.

Melanie loved chatting with her dad. After her parents' divorce, she'd lived with her Mom, but visited Vermont whenever she could. Both her parents were great in their own ways.

Her Mom was like a powerhouse in heels - smart, stunning, and crazy successful. She had this laser focus that helped her crush it at work, but sometimes made it hard for her to unwind. For Mom, a crazy night meant snuggling up with a good book or dominating her friends in a fierce game of Mah Jong. Different from Melanie's style, but still cool.

Dad, on the other hand, was a walking comedy show. He could find joy in a rainy day, and Melanie had definitely caught that bug.

Melanie felt like she'd lucked out, getting the best of both worlds. Mom's drive and Dad's humor? Talk about a winning combo. She was determined to keep that balance - work hard, but always make time for laughter.

"Your Mom's been calling me non-stop, too," Howard chuckled. "She's convinced you'll get lost, kidnapped, or worse. She even made me promise to send you a care package full of maps, snacks, and a first-aid kit."

Melanie couldn't help but smile at her mother's overprotective nature. "That sounds like Mom. Always prepared for anything."

"You know, when we first got married, she made me promise to always carry a map in the car, even though I insisted I knew my way around. She said, 'Howard, you may think you know everything, but even the wisest man can get lost sometimes.'"

"How did you two end up getting married, anyway? I mean, aside from Aunty Ah Lam playing matchmaker." Melanie's curiosity was piqued.

Howard smiled as he reminisced. "Would you believe it was my dashing good looks and charm?" He joked. "But honestly, your mother was the most intelligent and beautiful woman I'd ever met. Our marriage may have been arranged, but I fell head over heels for her."

"So, what changed?" Melanie asked.

Howard sighed. "We grew apart. But, you know, one thing never changed - our love for you. Your mother moved back to Singapore and remarried, but she's still the same strong, caring woman I married. And now, she's got a successful banker husband who dotes on her endlessly."

"And I'm married to a broken-down old horse," Howard added.

"Hey now, don't let Fran catch you talking like that. She might be from Brooklyn, but she's got ears like a bat," Melanie chuckled.

Fran DeDonato was a feisty Brooklyn woman who didn't hesitate to knock the teeth out of anyone who smarted off to her.

"Tell me about it. Yesterday Fran threatened to whack me. Again." Howard rolled his eyes. "All I did was remark that the pizza she made was a little dry."

"Oh, Dad. What were you thinking? You know better than to mess with a Brooklyn girl's cooking!" Melanie gasped.

"I know. I went temporarily insane."

Melanie laughed and glanced at the thinning traffic. "Alright, Dad, I better make my escape while I can. I'll call you when I hit Las Vegas."

"Okay, pumpkin. Be careful. Drive safe, you hear?"

"Careful is my middle name. Love you, Dad." Melanie had barely hung up when her phone buzzed again. The screen flashed "Rhonda Miltmore" - her soon-to-be boss in Vermont.

Melanie raised an eyebrow. "Talk about timing," she muttered, then answered, "Hello, Mrs. Miltmore. Everything okay?"

"Melanie, dear!" Rhonda's voice crackled through, a mix of worry and hope. "You're still coming, aren't you? You didn't have second thoughts about being my live-in nurse?"

Melanie couldn't help but smile at the older woman's concern.

"Absolutely, Mrs. Miltmore. In fact, I'm about to hit the road right now. Los Angeles is in my rearview mirror, and Vermont is--"

"I'm a dying woman, Melanie. I don't know how much time I have left. Weeks... maybe days." Rhonda let out a sick cough that didn't sound very sick at all—at least not to Melanie. "I'm seeing Dr. Richardson today. I fear the worst. Betty is anxious to leave...I need you at my side as soon as possible."

"I promise I'm on my way, Mrs. Miltmore," Melanie assured her.

"Melanie, your father and I go way back. When he suggested you come to work for me, I knew an angel was sending me the right nurse. Please don't delay. I'm a very sick woman. I don't know how much time I have left." Rhonda coughed again. A cough that sounded a little... rehearsed.

Was Rhonda Miltmore really dying? Absolutely not. The woman was the world's most notorious hypochondriac. She collected imaginary diseases like it was her job. At this rate, she'd probably outlive Melanie. Yet, the woman was willing to pay top dollar for a live-in nurse. And who was Melanie to turn down a well-paying gig?

"I'm on my way, Mrs. Miltmore. I promise."

"Wonderful," Rhonda perked up. "I'm anxious to see you... and oh, before I forget, I need to tell you that your job might be a smidge busier than we discussed. My son, Brent, hurt his leg. As you know Brent lives on the estate with me now. He's going to need medical care too. I will pay extra, of course."

Melanie's stomach did a little flip. Brent Miltmore? The jerk from eighth grade she'd decked for calling her a name? Oh, joy.

But she pushed those thoughts aside. "No problem at all, Mrs. Miltmore," Melanie said cheerfully. "I'm happy to help you and your son."

"I better go, Mrs. Miltmore. I have a long drive to Vermont. When I arrive in Snowy Oaks, I'll call you."

"Please do, dear. Safe travels!"

Melanie ended the call. The backseat of her SUV and the hatchback were so packed, they looked ready to birth a smaller car. Taking a deep breath, Melanie closed her eyes and thought, "Alright, you overstuffed metal beast, let's do this. May the road ahead be filled with new opportunities, hope, and laughter. And if we break down, may it be near a charming small town with a handsome mechanic who moonlights as a gourmet chef."

She opened her eyes, grinned, and added, "But seriously, please don't break down. I don't think my bank account could handle a new transmission right now."

Melanie tried to leave, but couldn't. The road was packed with cars. "Guess my big exit will have to wait," she laughed. She turned up her jazz music and nodded along while she waited. She knew it might take forever to get out of town, but she didn't mind. She was happy just sitting there, enjoying her music. Even when things were slow, Melanie found a way to enjoy life.

What Melanie didn't know was that a grumpy heart was waiting to rain on her in Vermont.

Chapter 2

Brent Miltmore

"**N**o!" Brent slammed the stainless-steel lid down hard. "This quiche is awful! I wanted soufflé! A PROPER SOUFFLÉ!"

John North took a deep breath. Being Rhonda's butler, cook, driver, and gardener was tough work. At almost seventy, John was ready to retire. He only stayed because he'd worked for Rhonda for over forty years. John had been there when Brent was born and had basically raised that little brat all on his own. Now, John felt old and tired. He just wanted to spend his days fishing.

"The soufflé is perfect, Brent," John said, unimpressed with the tantrum.

"In your dreams they are!" Brent glared up at a gray-headed man who seemed to have the ability to look into his soul. "Just forget it, John. I'm not hungry anyway."

"You best eat. Your pain medication works better with food. You'll get sick--"

"I know, John. Stop treating me like a kid!" Brent crossed his arms over a fancy white sweater that cost more than he has common sense.

There sat Brent: good-looking, rich, and successful. A real catch, right? Well, not exactly. Sure, he had the looks that made women stare. His blond hair and movie star face got attention. A face that made John think of the old actor, Paul Newman. And yeah, he made big bucks as a stockbroker. But the guy was a cold fish—a flat out cold fish! Heartless. Selfish. Cold. Brent only cared about himself and his golf score. At thirty-five, the guy was destined to become Ebeneezer Scrooge.

"You're acting like a toddler." John shook his head. "Here you sit in this fancy bedroom bigger than most houses people own. And look at you... throwing a fit over a soufflé."

"Excuse me?" Brent snapped, glaring at John. "Do I need to remind you that you are hired help?"

"Boy, I fought with your daddy in Vietnam!" John wanted to knock some sense into Brent, but knew it wouldn't work. "I was your daddy's best man. When your daddy died, I made a promise to never leave your momma's side. Hired help? The only one who needs help here is you!"

Brent knew his mother loved John like a brother. John had no family of his own, having grown up in an orphanage. But right now, Brent didn't care. "Get out," he growled.

John grabbed the food cart handle. "One of these days, someone's gonna teach you a lesson about that smart mouth of yours," he said. "And I'm gonna sit back and enjoy the show."

"I said GET OUT!" Brent yelled, his face turning red.

"Your daddy was a good man and your momma is an angel in

my view. But you? You're a sour bean, boy, let me tell you. A sour bean." John pushed the cart out, muttering about an ungrateful rich boy.

As the door closed, Brent heard John add, "Maybe we should've left him in the woods as a baby. Might've been raised better by wolves."

"Learn to iron your uniform, too!" Brent yelled after John, like a kid trying to get the last word.

John just rolled his eyes and kept walking. He'd heard better comebacks from a parrot.

"Moron," Brent muttered, flopping back on his bed. It was so soft and covered in pillows, it was like lying on a cloud. Not that Brent noticed or cared.

The glass doors to his balcony were wide open. A cool autumn breeze danced in, fresh and clean. Outside, the hills rolled on forever, covered in bright red and golden leaves.

Was Brent thankful for this perfect morning? Nope. He was too busy being grumpy to notice anything good. If happiness knocked on his door, he'd probably tell it to go away.

Brent grabbed his fancy phone and barked at his latest temporary secretary, "Fax the Whitfield account to my home office now!" The poor woman on the other end probably wished she could fax herself to a new job.

Brent went through secretaries like most people go through socks. No one in Snowy Oaks wanted to work for him. They'd rather wrestle a bear. Good thing his clients were in big cities and didn't know better.

Brent was smart, no doubt. He'd made it big on Wall Street. But being smart doesn't mean being nice. After his girlfriend ran off with his business partner and had his heart ripped out, Brent moved back home to Snowy Oaks.

He told himself it was a smart move. His father was gone, his mother was always "sick," and the mansion was big enough to house his ego (barely). Plus, living with mother meant he had a built-in audience for his daily rants about the stock market.

Besides, Brent was set to inherit the whole estate when his mother kicked the bucket. Might as well start acting like the king of the castle now. Who needed friends, family, or love when you had a fat bank account, good looks and a killer golf swing?

"Yes, Mr. Miltmore. Right away, sir," a skittish girl promised Brent as she scribbled 'Whitfield' on a yellow legal pad.

"ASAP!" Brent barked, hanging up just as his mother walked in.

Rhonda Miltmore was a tall and scrawny woman with short gray hair. Scrawny or not, Rhonda Miltmore was healthier than a horse. Rhonda kind of looked like Bee Arthur to Brent. Many women Rhonda's age reminded Brent of Bee Arthur for some reason. Brent called them 'Copy and Paste Carrots.' Oh, deep down Brent guessed he loved his mother. Why not? The woman had always been good to him. It was just that she was always so sick—or at least claiming to be sick.

"What's the drama today, mother?" Brent sighed. "Are you dying, or just planning your funeral... again?"

"I heard you yell at John. I will not tolerate you being rude to that man," Rhonda snapped. She narrowed her eyes and folded her skinny arms over a deep blue blouse. "I'm still in charge of this estate, John."

"Fine, I'll leave then," Brent shot back.

"Not with a hurt leg, you won't." Rhonda studied John's right leg. His leg wasn't in a cast. Brent's right food had struck a hidden root on a nature trail he had been jogging on. A bad fall and a twisted knee followed. A blue ice pack was sitting on Brent's right knee.

"My knee, mother, my knee. Not my leg," Brent groaned. "I twisted my knee. I'll be fine in a few days."

"Will you?" Rhonda raised an eyebrow. "Dr. Edwards seemed pretty worried about those x-rays."

"Great, now I'm dying!" Brent threw his hands up. "Should we call the funeral home or just dump me in the backyard?"

"There's no need to be snippy, young man!" Rhonda hated to admit it but her son was a snot. A spoiled snot. She could barely stand to be in the same room with her son. "I've noticed that Carly hasn't come to visit you."

"Why would she? We haven't seen each other in weeks."

"You two broke up?" Rhonda frowned.

"We were never a thing, mother," Brent groaned, rolling his eyes. Rhonda was always trying to get him married off to some goofball or another. Carly Troesh had been the most recent lab mouse. Brent had suffered through exactly three dates with her. Three. That was his limit. After date number three, he sent Carly packing. Carly was more than happy to give Brent his own set of walking papers.

"I went out with Carly as a favor to you, mother. Carly was new in town and your friend's kid. It was charity work, basically."

"But Carly was so sweet-" Rhonda started.

"Yeah, and she laughed like a hyena with the hiccups," Brent cut in.

Rhonda sighed, probably wondering where she'd gone wrong. "I would like grandchildren before I die, Brent."

"You're not dying. You're never going to die, mother!" Brent rolled his eyes again. At this rate, he was going to strain something. "Your mother is still living, for goodness sake. You're gonna outlive us all."

"You know what I mean, Brent. It's time for you to settle down and get married." Rhonda decided to take a soft approach.

Brent loved to argue. Being on the defense gave Brent the excuse to play the victim. Rhonda wasn't going to allow that. All she wanted was grandkids. Was that too much to ask? No!

But boy, getting a grandchild from Brent was like trying to use a feather to carve through a hard piece of stone.

"Don't start, mother. I'm not in the mood. I can't even get a decent soufflé around here."

"Now, Brent," Rhonda eased onto a plush sitting chair, "let's be reasonable. You're not getting any younger. It's time you settled down and began a family of your own."

Good grief. All Brent wanted to do was ice his knee in peace. Was that too much to ask? Now he had to sit through another 'Drilling' episode and listen to his mother squawk about not having grandchildren.

The idea of ever having kids made Brent want to crawl into a deep hole. Kids were loud, messy, and expensive - three things Brent hated. If he had kids, goodbye golf weekends and hello diaper duty. No more zooming around in his Lamborghini - he'd be stuck driving a minivan covered in sticky handprints. Kids were definitely not in Brent's life plan, right between "learn to cook" and "be nice to people."

"Uh, before we talk about marriage, mother, did you find a replacement for Betty?" Brent desperately fired off a foul hook hoping his mother would take the bait.

"I did. Melanie Jenkins will begin working as my new live-in nurse," Rhonda answered. "Melanie once lived in Snowy Oaks. You might remember her?"

Brent's forehead wrinkled up. Melanie Jenkins. Now where had he heard that name before? Brent thought for a minute. Melanie Jenkins? Why did that name ring a bell? Suddenly, it hit him like a ton of bricks. Or more accurately, like a fist to the nose.

"That's the girl who broke my nose in eighth grade!" he yelled, touching his nose like it might still be sore.

"Oh Brent, you were just kids," Rhonda said, waving it off.

"Just kids?" Brent threw the ice pack on his knee off and tried to stand up. He winced in pain and decided to remain sitting. "I had to have nose surgery because of that... that... criminal Amazonian nutcase!"

"Brent, you chose to get a nose job at twenty-five. There was no medical reason for you--"

"This coming from a woman who claims she's dying from the moment she wakes up until the moment she goes to bed!"

Rhonda winced. "Well, I have my... issues."

"I can't believe you hired a criminal!" Brent huffed, his face turning an alarming shade of red. "What's next? Hiring a car thief as your chauffeur?"

"Brent--" Rhonda tried to interject.

"Fire her at once!" he demanded, puffing out his chest as if he were the CEO of the household.

"I will not," Rhonda objected. "Howard Jenkins is a dear friend to this family. He recommended his daughter to me."

"But mother--" Brent continued to whine.

"Melanie comes highly recommended, Brent. She is a skilled and qualified nurse," Rhonda countered, her tone steady and firm.

Brent touched his nose again, like he was checking if it was still there. "She probably moonlights as the Grim Reaper for her patients."

Rhonda sighed. So much for talking about grandchildren. "Brent, as much as I hate to admit this, not many nurses are willing to care for me. I can be...difficult at times. On top of that, I insist that my nurse live right here on the estate in the guest house. Melanie has agreed to everything and--"

"And finish off what she started in the eighth grade!" Brent winced, remembering that day. In his mind, he saw the face of an angry girl, then a fist, then stars. "I bled for days. I nearly died."

"You did not almost die." Rhonda looked at her son. "If I recall, you were the one who called Melanie a very ugly name."

"Mother, I'm the victim here. I was the one who was assaulted and nearly died," Brent moaned, his voice dripping with self-pity.

"You got punched in the nose by an angry eighth grader, Brent. Not run over by a truck." Rhonda said, standing up.

"I'm not going to fire Melanie. Melanie has been working as a nurse at a very busy trauma hospital in Los Angeles for eleven years. She has solid medical experience--"

"Yeah. Yeah. Go bore John with the details." Brent grumbled, still poking at his nose like it was a new toy. "Tell John to pack my bags. I'm out of here."

"You are not going anywhere." Rhonda stomped her foot down onto a soft brown carpet. "Look at you! You're in a bedroom fit for a king, acting like a cranky toddler who missed nap time. Well, Brent, I won't have that! Do you hear me? Grow up and be a man for once in your life!" Rhonda stormed out of the bedroom, probably to find some aspirin.

Brent ignored her. "My nose. That awful Amazonian moose broke my nose."

In his head, he replayed the scene from eighth grade: "You stupid moose! Where'd you get those antlers?" Then, bam! The girl with the funny hair turned into Muhammad Ali, and his nose turned into mush.

Okay. So maybe Brent had called Melanie an ugly name. Maybe he had also been at fault for teasing the girl about her hair for weeks. Maybe he had pushed Melanie to her breaking point. But so what? Melanie had punched Brent right in the nose!

And now the vicious brute was going to be his mother's new nurse and live on the property? It was like hiring a shark as a lifeguard!

Brent desperately tried to think. Would Melanie remember him? Of course, she would, he thought. After all, he was Brent Miltmore, local legend (in his own mind). No woman could forget him - or at least that's what he told himself in the mirror every morning. Melanie would remember him.

"Maybe she took this job to finish what she started in eighth grade," he muttered. "Who knows? But I'm not sticking around to let Wonder Woman break my nose again. I'm outta here!"

Brent managed to stand up. He stumbled to his closet. "I'll go live on my father's yacht," he declared to his shoes.

Suddenly, someone cleared their throat. Brent spun around like a clumsy ballerina to see John in the doorway.

"Your momma says to tie you down if you try to leave," John said, cool as a cucumber. "So why don't you park yourself back on that bed before I have to get creative with some rope?"

"I'm out of here!" Brent yelled, acting like a petulant child. "Melanie Jenkins is a certified nut job! You have no idea what she did to me!"

"You ain't going nowhere." John tossed up a set of car keys and grinned. "That fancy car of yours just so happens to be out of gas, too."

"Hey, those are my keys!" Brent lunged at John like a bad action movie hero. But his knee had other plans, sending him crashing to the floor with all the grace of a sack of potatoes.

John could only shake his head. "Doc said to walk when you can. Not fall down."

Brent watched John walk away. He gritted his teeth and hit the floor with a hard fist. "Come back with my car keys! Do you hear me? Do you HEAR ME!"

Downstairs, Rhonda heard Brent's incessant yelling and got a sneaky grin on her face. She leaned back in her chair, her eyes glinting with mischief as she murmured, "Oh, I hear you, my dear son. And I'm starting to get some ideas..."

Chapter 3

The Meeting

Melanie cruised down Snow Owl Lane, feeling like she'd driven straight into a postcard. The road hugged Blustery Wind Lake, which sparkled like it was showing off. The trees were decked out in their fall finest.

Melanie nearly ran off the road a few times, too busy gawking at the scenery. The air smelled like hayrides, apple cider, and warm donuts. "Pinch me, I must be dreaming!" she laughed.

Snow Owl Lane turned into Burch Manor Road which continued further north, running past rolling hills and diamond shaped little lakes. Hay bales sat out on the hills for cows to come munch on. The hills, like the lake, were surrounded by every autumn beauty Melanie could dream of.

Burch Manor Road ended at a tall iron gate that required a security code to open. Melanie pulled up to an intercom that was probably smarter than her phone. She pressed a glowing green button and waited.

"Melanie?" a sick voice asked. Well, a sick voice that wasn't as sick as it sounded.

"It's me, Mrs. Miltmore," Melanie answered.

"Oh good. I'll open the gate. Drive to the main house," Mrs. Miltmore said, then added with all the drama of a soap opera star, "And do hurry. I think I feel a fainting spell coming on!"

Melanie thought to herself, "This job is going to be... interesting."

Melanie sat back and took a minute to check herself as the iron gate began to slowly creak open. "Gray and green scrubs? Check. Neutral colors, just like my personality," she joked to herself. She glanced in the rearview mirror. Her bangs were curled up in small waves. Somewhat dorky but acceptable. Melanie didn't care what people thought. "Hair is good. Lip gloss is good. No perfume. Just in case Mrs. Miltmore has allergies. Check, check and check. Let's move."

Melanie drove up a long winding concrete driveway that led to a huge picturesque manor like it had jumped straight out of a fairy tale. The driveway made a circle, allowing Melanie to park in front of the manor directly behind a lovely marble fountain that was probably worth more than her entire life savings. Boy. Talk about money. Mr. Miltmore had been one rich guy. All Melanie could do was whistle to herself. "What a place."

The grounds surrounding the manor were so perfect, lush and filled with flower beds full of autumn flowers. Melanie didn't spot one single blade of grass that looked out of place. Behind the manor stood a large pool, a pool house, a green house and a guest house. Somewhere on the property, there was a horse stable. Melanie wasn't sure where. She guessed Rhonda would tell her.

A set of thick, shiny, cherry wood doors slowly opened and out stepped a man who had to be John. "Ms. Jenkins?" he called.

"That's me!" Melanie chirped, hopping out of her car with all the grace of an excited puppy.

What a breath of fresh air. A happy heart instead of a depressed soul. The nurse Melanie was replacing had been enough to make an army of clowns want to jump off a bridge. John smiled and said, "Mrs. Miltmore is waiting in the parlor. I have coffee and cookies waiting."

"Great, let me grab my medical bag and we'll be all set." Melanie hurried to retrieve her gear and then made her way up a set of marble steps. "This is some place. I grew up in Snowy Oaks but this is the first time I've been out to the Miltmore Estate."

"It's nice alright. But you get used to it over time." John studied Melanie's face for a second. What he saw warmed his heart. A cheerful soul. "I'll show you to the guest house when you get finished with Mrs. Miltmore."

"Great," Melanie exclaimed excitedly.

"This way." John ushered Melanie into a foyer that could double as an art museum. "I like to air the place out," he said, locking the doors. "Otherwise, it starts to smell like old money and broken dreams."

Melanie gaped at the surroundings. "Whoa, did they buy Buckingham Palace and ship it over?"

"You can get lost in here, that's for sure." John smiled. "Maybe I should have drawn you out a map."

"Maybe," Melanie smiled back.

"Follow me." John led Melanie to a cozy parlor that looked like it was plucked from an Agatha Christie novel. The parlor was impressive in size but not as bathed with money signs as the rest of the manor. Rhonda was resting on a green sitting chair, basking in the warmth of a fireplace that probably cost more than Melanie's entire apartment.

"Mrs. Miltmore, your new nurse, Melanie Jenkins, is here," John announced.

"Thank you, John."

John winked at Melanie. "She wants everything to look all fancy. I'll be in the kitchen," he whispered.

"Okay," Melanie winked back.

"Please, Melanie, sit down," Rhonda urged once John left.

A second sitting chair was facing the fireplace. Melanie happily sat down. "This is a lovely parlor."

"My favorite room," Rhonda told Melanie. She coughed. The cough sounded weak. "My doctor claims there's nothing wrong with me. Doctors don't know everything."

Melanie sized up Rhonda. Rhonda was wearing a dark green dress. Fancy but not overdone. Her skin color was good. Body language is a little tense but nothing horrible. Eyes clear. Voice clear.

"Well, I'll create my own medical chart. I'll record your blood pressure and temperature every two hours, four times a day. From what I've seen, your blood pressure is really good--"

"I'm more concerned with the fatigue, headaches, dizzy spells, chills and... well, you'll see," Rhonda said, sounding like she was reading off a WebMD checklist.

"You're not on any medications other than a low dose antidepressant, right?"

"I take my vitamins and honey everyday along with an aspirin."

"Good." Melanie offered a caring smile.

Rhonda wanted to smile back but didn't. Melanie was very pretty and her smile was as sweet as honey—but she looked so... so... well, dorky. Dorky? Rhonda hated to apply that word to Melanie but she couldn't help it. Maybe it was the large eye glasses or the way Melanie's bangs were? At least the woman wasn't covered from head to toe with tattoos. Tattoos wouldn't have mattered. There was no way Brent was going to fall for a woman like Melanie. One look at the woman told Rhonda all she needed to know. Still, she had to try.

"You're very pretty," Rhonda said.

"I'm also nearly halfway to forty. I figure by the time I'm fifty I'll be bald." Melanie hoped Rhonda would smile at her joke. Rhonda didn't smile. Ouch. "Just a little joke."

"I see. I'm sorry if I'm not in a humorous mood. I have a lot on my mind." Rhonda looked at the fireplace. Should she begin baiting Melanie or wait? She decided to toss a little cheese out. "Melanie, I'm getting older and I don't have any grandchildren. I could die at any time. All I want is to be a grandmother. My son—my only child—is all alone in the world. Lost. Sad. Desperate for love."

Desperate for love? Oh boy. Was that a whopper or what.

Melanie knew who Brent Miltmore was. She had punched the guy in the nose for calling her a stupid moose. Melanie wasn't the violent type but when a girl is pushed to her limits, she lets her fist do her talking.

Melanie could only pray that Brent had changed through the years. From what she had learned from her Dad, the guy was still pretty much the same. "Love is tough, Mrs. Miltmore--"

"Call me Rhonda, dear."

"Okay. Rhonda it is." Melanie tried to relax the best she could. Why not? She wasn't about to start a stressful twelve-hour shift at a fast-paced hospital filled with gunshot wounds, heart attacks, bodies mangled from car accidents or stabbings. Nah. Melanie had what she called a 'Cream Pie' gig. Nice and peaceful. One patient. Simple task. Easy hours. Good pay. "Thanks, Dad," Melanie thought to herself. "You're the best."

Only if Melanie knew that her new boss was planning to play Cupid with a broken arrow.

Rhonda eyed Melanie, mentally giving her a makeover. A new hairstyle, stylish glasses, some nice makeup and Melanie would be a real doll. In time. Rhonda didn't want to scare off her new nurse.

"I have the guest house all set. The carpets have been shampooed. New furniture has been put in along with a new bed. There's cable and internet and plenty of hot water."

"Great. I can't wait to get settled in." Melanie offered an excited smile. She was on contract for one whole year. After that? Well, she would wait and see what surprises life threw at her next. "I have my luggage and some lunch stuff in my SUV. But first," Melanie eased off her smile and tried to force a professional appearance to show up, "I would like to create your medical chart. Your last nurse, from what I saw, didn't keep a very good record of your daily vitals."

Rhonda watched Melanie open a brown medical bag and pull out a blood pressure machine—the old, old... very old... fashioned kind. "Betty used the kind that wrapped around my arm."

"Those are okay but I prefer to listen. You get a better reading that way, in my opinion." Melanie stood up. "I'll take your temp after I check your blood pressure."

Brent burst into the parlor just as Melanie began to attach a blood pressure cuff to Rhonda's right arm. His knee was somewhat better but he was hobbling around with a cane, looking cranky.

"I want to make one thing perfectly clear. You are to stay away from me at all times!" he ordered Melanie in a stern tone. "My mother made it clear that she has asked you to take care of my knee. You are not to come within a hundred yards of my knee. Or my nose. Is that clear?"

Melanie, cool as a cucumber, ignored Brent while she took Rhonda's blood pressure. When she was on duty her mind was like a steel trap. "114/74." Melanie checked Rhonda's pulse. Brent watched. "Sixty-one. Outstanding. Let me take your temp."

Brent couldn't stop staring at Melanie. Talk about a blast from the past. The girl he teased in eighth grade looked like she'd been frozen in time. Her bangs were a disaster - did she cut them with a butter knife? And those glasses - thick as soda bottles. Brent looked her up and down, trying to find one nice thing to say. No luck. Melanie was about as attention-gabbing as oatmeal – plain, not even the fancy kind with fruit.

"98.1. Great." Melanie put her equipment away and then fished out a brown folder from her medical bag. She sat back down and opened the folder. "It's almost eleven o'clock. I'll take your vitals again around one o'clock."

Rhonda watched Melanie record her vitals. Melanie was very professional. That was good. Rhonda glanced back at her son. The way Brent was looking at Melanie made Rhonda's heart sink. That wasn't good. "Brent, leave us alone."

"Just make sure you stand clear of me," Brent ordered Melanie. "I remember what you did to me--"

"I heard you the first time, Mr. Miltmore. You can leave us now," Melanie cut Brent off in a professional—but scolding—voice that impressed Rhonda. "I don't like being disturbed when I'm taking care of a patient."

Ouch. Melanie scolded Brent. No one scolded Brent. "Leave," Rhonda ordered her son before he could run his mouth at Melanie.

Brent left in a huff. Okay, so Melanie wasn't actually out to get him. Big deal. He'd had time to think about how he'd reacted, and man, did he feel dumb. Silly? Nah. Irrational? Getting warmer. How about just plain paranoid and ridiculous? Yep, that's the ticket. And somehow, this was all Melanie's fault too. Add it to the list of reasons she annoyed him. Brent would find a way to get back at her. Someday. Maybe after he learned to chill out a bit.

Melanie waited for the parlor door to close before speaking.

"Rhonda, your vitals are great. I want to have some blood work done on you. I want to start from scratch and monitor you over the next year to see if there are any major changes."

"Oh, well, of course." Rhonda said, her spirits lifting slightly. New blood work. She liked the sound of that. "I have been feeling very weak. My appetite isn't very good, either." Rhonda coughed again. Not a very convincing cough but a cough nonetheless.

Melanie smiled in her heart. Rhonda has a reputation for being a grand hypochondriac. That was okay. The woman looked sweet enough and probably meant well. "I'll make an appointment to see your doctor."

"Very well. If you think that's best," Rhonda agreed.

"I do." Melanie looked down at Rhonda. She wasn't about to let a jerk like Brent get under her skin. "I'm sorry I had to ask your son to leave. I don't like being disturbed when I'm taking care of a patient. Your health is very important to me. I need to remain focused at all times without being distracted."

"I'm sorry my son came across so rude. I don't know what gets into him?" Rhonda apologized.

Melanie chuckled and said, "It seems your son remembers the little fight we had years back in the eighth grade. Well, the past is the past. Water under the bridge, fist under the nose. What matters now is that you receive the best medical care that I can possibly offer."

Rhonda felt so grateful to have Melanie as her nurse. Betty stunk eggs. "Uh, do you have anybody in your life?" she dared to ask Melanie.

"Are you asking if I'm single?" Melanie asked. Rhonda nodded. "Yep. I'm a single jingle," Melanie grinned. "But who knows? The right guy might show up when I least expect it."

"Good. I mean... yes, of course. A little optimism never hurts, dear," Rhonda said, her eyes darting to the fire like it held the secrets of the universe. Melanie was single. Good. Perfect.

The only question was... how could she play matchmaker for Melanie and Brent? It would be like trying to mix oil and water. Those two were as different as night and day. Melanie, with her DIY haircut and oversized glasses. Brent? More like a walking country club brochure. She smiled, he scowled. She laughed, he whined. Melanie saw the bright side of a rainy day, while Brent only cared if his golf clubs were color-coordinated and his score was under par.

And to spice things up, Melanie had once rearranged Brent's nose with her fist back in the day. Apparently, Brent still hadn't gotten over it. He held onto that grudge like it was his most prized possession, constantly bringing it up and acting like it happened yesterday.

"Mind if I have some coffee and cookies?" Melanie asked.

"Of course. Have all the coffee and cookies you want. We'll sit and chat for a while."

Melanie smiled. Yep. She has a 'Cream Pie' coffee. Sitting and talking with Rhonda and getting paid to do so was nice. No more long shifts. No more coming home with sore legs and blisters on her feet. No more snotty doctors and overcrowded exam rooms. No more running herself silly. Nope. For the next year, Melanie was going to take it easy and focus on one single patient and drink coffee and eat cookies doing it. The only problem Melanie foresaw was a jerk named Brent Miltmore.

That was okay. Melanie had already punched Brent once, and she'd do it again in a heartbeat. It was no wonder Rhonda was so depressed. What woman in her right mind would ever want to marry a donkey like Brent and have children with the guy. Poor Rhonda was up a river without a paddle. Oh, well. That wasn't Melanie's problem. Not her circus, not her monkeys.

If Melanie could've peeked into Rhonda's brain right then, she'd have sprinted away. But nope, she was clueless about the tornado of terrible ideas spinning in there.

Ah, love. It's like a rollercoaster – thrilling, scary, and it might make you hurl.

Chapter 4

Dinner

The guest house was a dream. Three cozy bedrooms. Two bathrooms. A living room that made you want to live there forever. And the kitchen? Chef's kiss. Boy, it was like living in a dream. Melanie bounced around like a kid on a sugar rush, checking out her new digs, unaware that a pair of cold eyes were watching the guest house from a shadowy window. Mr. Grumpy Pants himself, Brent, was doing his best creeper impression, staring at the guest house with steam coming from his ears. "Little Miss Sunshine has everybody fooled. Not me. I remember. Oh, I remember."

Rhonda entered Brent's bedroom. She saw her son standing beside the bedroom window clutching his wooden cane with an angry hand.

"Dinner is ready," she announced.

"I'm not hungry," Brent grumbled.

Rhonda bit down on her lower lip. She had to get Brent in the same room with Melanie.

"You look very nice in that brown sweater, son. The color brown has always complimented you," Rhonda remarked.

"Stop it, mother. I'd rather cancel my golf trip than sit through a meal with her. Actually, make that my next two trips," Brent protested.

"Melanie is a delightful woman, Brent." Rhonda walked to her son. She looked out of the bedroom window. The guest house came into view. "Brent, that stuff is ancient history. You and Melanie are both thirty-five years old. It's been twenty-one years since--"

"Twenty-one hard years," Brent sneered.

"Oh, you're being impossible." Rhonda wanted to slap her son. She held back. A mother had a way of being able to pick up a heavy rug and peek under. "Brent, you were always a difficult child. I blame myself for that. Your poor father warned me that I was spoiling you. But you are my only child. I only wanted to see you happy."

Brent ignored Rhonda.

"You've grown into a difficult man," Rhonda continued. "I understand why. Your father drowned at sea when you were only sixteen. Lara betrayed you when you were twenty-four--"

Brent slowly turned his head and looked at his mother. "Don't ever mention that woman's name to me again."

Rhonda sighed. "Your best friend betrayed you," she continued. "You have many reasons to be hurt and bitter. I understand that. But honey," Rhonda reached out and touched Brent's arm, "there comes a time when you have to realize that being willing to heal is better than remaining stuck in a dark hole."

"This coming from a woman who claims she's dying all the time, right?"

Rhonda sighed again. "Perhaps, Brent," she confessed, "I have my own ways of dealing with pain. Losing your father killed me. I continued to live for you. But maybe... I want to be sick because if I am, I'll be closer to being with your father again."

Rhonda's confession shocked Brent. He had never once considered that his mother's hypochondria was the result of intense grief. Before Brent could say a word, he saw the door to the guesthouse open. Melanie walked outside wearing a cheesy autumn dress covered with smiley faces. "Here she comes."

Rhonda watched Melanie start making her way up a cobblestone pathway. She winced when Melanie's dress became clearer and clearer. "Brent, come down for dinner. John made a delicious stew."

Brent had to admit that he was hungry. And John did make a great stew. Besides, why would Brent let a little flea like Melanie force him to remain trapped in his own bedroom? He was a man for crying out loud! A man! Not a sissy momma's boy. "Fine. I'll come down for dinner."

"Great." Rhonda spun away and left the bedroom before Brent could change his mind.

"Sure, I'll come down for dinner, mother," Brent grumbled. "But only because I need to get rid of a deranged moose. And trust me, this is one war I'm not going to lose." Brent's brain kept cooking up angry, bitter thoughts. A devious idea formed. "Maybe I will let Melanie Jenkins look at my knee and then sue her for making it worse. Mother will have to fire her. Boom, problem solved."

Brent stomped downstairs the way the Grinch made his way into Whoville on Christmas Eve. By the time he reached the dining room, Melanie was already seated at a long table fit for a king. Lit candles complimented the table. Crystal water glasses were set out. Expensive—no, priceless—rare plates and bowls rested next to the water glasses. Oh, John had gone all out. "Take your place at the head of the table, honey," Rhonda told Brent, probably hoping he'd feel important enough to behave.

John grinned and excused himself as Brent took his seat. Rhonda was sitting to his left and Melanie—Ms. Smiley Dress—was sitting to his right; far too close for comfort. "The dining room looks grand," Melanie told Rhonda. "I love the drapes." Melanie had no intention of letting Brent ruin dinner.

Brent quickly cleared his throat. "Melanie, my mother had brought an important fact to my attention," he spoke in a cold voice. "What happened between us in the eighth grade is in the past. We're both adults now. We should act accordingly. Therefore, I will forgive you and let the past go."

"Good," Melanie smiled. "I'm glad to hear that."

Brent resisted the urge to throw a glass of cold water onto Melanie's nerdy dress. "I have also decided that I will allow you to check my knee from time to time."

Rhonda tensed up. Alarm bells began going off in her head. She knew her son's heart—boy did she. Brent was up to something. His eyes were grinning in a way that made Rhonda's heart sink. "Well, maybe it would be best if your doctor--"

"No, no, mother. I feel that Melanie is perfectly capable of checking on my knee from time to time. After all, she did work as an emergency room nurse for many years, did she not?" Brent asked. "I'm sure a twisted knee is nothing compared to gunshot wounds."

Melanie picked up a water glass. "I'll be happy to check your knee as needed, Mr. Miltmore."

"Please, Melanie, if we're going to be friends... call me Brent."

"Okay." Melanie took a sip of water. "So, Rhonda, the kitchen in the guest house is a dream. And the coffee maker... I never drooled over so much in my life."

Brent frowned. Melanie had shrugged him off without the least bit of concern or attention. No one shrugged Brent Miltmore off. "Mother, I would like us to go out on the yacht when my knee is healed. The water is divine this time of year. After we spend time on the water, we can have dinner at the yacht club. The drive to the coast will be nice. You can bring Melanie, of course."

Rhonda's heart sank ever deeper. Brent was up to no good. "Perhaps, Brent. We'll see how I feel. I do have a cough."

"The salt air will do you good," Brent insisted. "Melanie, have you ever been out on a yacht? Wait, what am I thinking? On your salary, all you can probably afford is a row boat. Please accept my apologies for asking such a silly question."

"I like row boats," Melanie kept her smile. "Back in Los Angeles, I owned a surfboard but never learned to surf. Nearly drowned myself a few times." Her laugh came out in that adorably awkward snort she could never quite control. "Ended up selling it to some kid for three bucks."

"How fascinating." Brent lifted his water glass, his Harvard class ring catching the light. He didn't trade billions on Wall Street by entertaining stories about failed surfing adventures and discount surfboards. Especially not from nurses who snorted when they laughed.

Melanie's smile widened, clearly enjoying herself. "Yeah, Roger got a great deal. That surfboard set me back three hundred bucks," she said.

Rhonda studied Brent's eyes as Melanie talked. Oh boy. Invisible poison was dripping out of her son's eyes. "Uh, Melanie, do you like the arts? The symphony perhaps?" she asked in a quick voice.

"I like jazz," Melanie answered. "I love Jimmy Dorsey."

Brent glared at Melanie. How could a thirty-five-year-old nurse dress like she'd borrowed clothes from a kindergartener's wardrobe? It was like watching a kid playing dress-up, except the kid forgot to stop for two decades. All the women Brent knew acted their age and dressed accordingly, but Melanie? She was trapped in a strange Twilight Zone episode where the body aged but the mind didn't.

"Do you like museums?" Rhonda asked in a hopeful voice.

"Not really. Museums are too stuffy for me," Melanie offered an honest answer. "My mother used to drag me to museums all the time when I was growing up. I liked to spend time on the beach playing volleyball or roller skating."

"Roller skating?" Rhonda cringed. This wouldn't end well.

"Sure. The Santa Monica beach path was perfect for it," Melanie beamed, blissfully unaware of how Brent would use this information. "Lots of cute guys to crash into."

Brent saw the perfect door open. "Melanie, are you married?"

"Not yet." Melanie took another sip of water. "Someday... if it's in the cards. But for now, I'm flying solo, enjoying the journey."

"Have you ever been engaged?" Brent asked.

Rhonda cleared her throat. "Brent, Melanie's personal life is not our concern--"

"No, that's okay, Rhonda. I don't mind answering Brent's question." Melanie began to swing her feet under the table.

"I've never been engaged. I had a few boyfriends but nothing serious. I dated a doctor once who turned out to be a total jerk. He only wanted my body. I punched him in the face."

Brent leaned back. "That seems to be a habit with you."

"Well, I did spend a night in jail," Melanie confessed. "But I always look on the bright side of things. I met a woman there who taught me how to cripple a man in two moves."

"Uh... how nice." Rhonda felt her brain short-circuit.

"Oh, Nadine was fantastic," Melanie chuckled. "She got arrested for trying to kill her husband. Seventh time! Quite the character." She snorted mid-laugh, completely unbothered.

Brent rolled his eyes. "Do you have any educated friends?"

"My best friend is a nurse and my landlord was a retired Vietnam Vet who earned his PhD in math," Melanie answered. "Wilson helped me with all the math I needed to pass nursing school. Honestly, I don't know what I would've done without him—I'm hopeless with numbers."

"I'm sure... *Wilson*... was more than happy to tutor you," Brent said, his voice laced with insinuation.

Brent's voice hinted at an area Melanie didn't like or respect. "Wilson has been happily married to his wife for over forty years. He and his wife practically adopted me as their own daughter."

"I'm sure he did," Brent murmured, taking a sip of water, clearly unimpressed. "So, you have never been married or engaged. And now you're living here working for my mother. May I ask what your future goals are, Melanie?"

Melanie felt her temper flare up but quickly tossed some cold water on the flame. Why let Brent get under her skin. "I intend to work out my contract and then see what happens," she said coolly. "If Rhonda wants me to stay on, great. If not, I'll pack up my stethoscope and hit the road. There's always another pulse to check somewhere."

Brent nodded, looking like he was listening to a kid explain how clouds are made of cotton candy. He thought he had Melanie right where he wanted her. Perfect. Just perfect. It was time to knock his enemy down a peg or two. "Mother and I will watch your performance very carefully, Melanie," he said, trying to sound important. "If mother and I decide your services are adequate, maybe we'll let you stick around. With that said, I want you to maintain a professional attitude at all times. And, oh, about your clothes? Let's try to dress like a grown-up, okay? No more raiding the kids' section for dinner outfits."

Rhonda's fingers gripped her napkin and stiffened in her chair.

"Melanie's dress is just fine. Brent."

"In this house, we dress like adults," Brent said. He took a sip of water, probably to wash down the taste of his own superiority. "Oh, and Melanie? I need you to check my knee after dinner. It's terribly swollen."

"Sure, no problem," Melanie replied smoothly, flashing him a quick, sarcastic smile. "But I'll need someone else present. John, or maybe you, Rhonda? It's not exactly professional for a woman to be alone with a male patient." Her gaze lingered on Brent, the smile never quite reaching her eyes.

"I would prefer to be alone when you check my knee--" Brent pulled out his boardroom voice.

"Sorry. Not going to happen." Melanie matched his tone with pure nurse authority.

Brent squinted. How was he supposed to destroy Melanie if he couldn't get her alone? "I must insist," he said, sounding like a kid demanding the last cookie. "I'm a very private person--"

"Look, Brent," Melanie cut him off, her voice sharp as a scalpel. "I'm not checking your knee unless someone else is in the room. I've worked in a busy ER. Plenty of guys have tried to pull me aside. I know how this game is played."

"Are you insinuating--" Brent asked, feeling offended.

"I'm not insinuating anything. I'm simply protecting myself," Melanie clarified.

"I'll be with you when you check my son's knee," Rhonda assured Melanie. "Now, move on to something more pleasant. Maybe a trip to the coast would be nice."

Brent glared at Melanie with daggers in his eyes. The woman was shooting him down at every step. "Just remember that you're the one who spent time in jail for assaulting a doctor," he snapped, trying to sound tough but coming off more like a grumpy toddler. He stood up, nearly knocking over his chair in his rush to look dramatic. "You know what? I take back my offer. I wouldn't let you check my knee if you were the last nurse on Earth. I'd rather Google my symptoms and hope for the best."

"Brent--" Rhonda interjected, attempting to diffuse the tension.

"Mother, where'd you find this... walking cartoon?" Brent snapped, his voice dripping with more sarcasm. "Did you pick her up at a yard sale? Look at her! She looks like a silly clown for crying out loud! Why can't you hire real professionals instead of someone who looks like they got dressed in the dark?"

Brent stormed out - well, more like hobbled dramatically - before anyone could respond. In his head, he was making a grand exit. In reality, he looked like a penguin with a grudge.

"Stupid moose," he muttered, heading upstairs. "I hope she falls in the pool and sinks to the bottom."

Flopping onto his bed like a dramatic teenager, Brent started plotting. "How do I get rid of her? Maybe I could take her out on the lake and... Nah, orange isn't my color, and I don't think I'd enjoy prison food. Think, Brent. Think."

And Brent did think. Oh boy, did he. An hour later, another Grinch smile covered his face. "That's it. I'll plant some money in the guest house and call the cops. Perfect!"

John was standing outside Brent's bedroom door. He heard

Brent talking to himself. "That boy just ain't no good!" John muttered, scurrying off to tattle to Rhonda.

When Rhonda heard, she rested her chin on her hands. "John, how can we make these two fall for each other?"

John stared at her like she'd grown a second head. "Rhonda, you're crazy if you think Brent is ever going to fall for a woman like Melanie. That boy just ain't no good I'm telling you. No good at all."

"He's my son, John. I can't give up on him yet and, somehow, I'm starting to feel that Melanie is just the pill Brent needs to take."

Meanwhile, Melanie was outside, stargazing.

Brent limped to his window, spotting Melanie. "Your days are numbered," he grumbled, sounding more like a cartoon villain than a grown man.

But as Brent stared at Melanie, the strangest thing happened. The way Melanie was standing there, hair dancing in the breeze, she actually looked... pretty.

"No way! Not happening! If anyone ever finds out I had a crush on her in school, I'll never be able to live it down." He shook his head hard, trying to knock the weird thought out of his brain. "I have to get rid of her!"

Chapter 5

The War Begins

R honda sat up all night thinking. When morning arrived, she awoke feeling worn down and exhausted. Rhonda rubbed her temples, wondering how on earth she was going to get these two stubborn hearts to even consider the possibility of love.

Brent was dead set on getting Melanie out of the picture, no matter what it took. Melanie, on the other hand, couldn't care less about Brent. To her, he was just another part of the job, and not even an interesting one at that. She had zero interest in him as a person, let alone as a potential love interest.

To make matters worse, Brent had orchestrated a plan to land Melanie behind bars. Talk about holding a grudge! As Charlie Brown would say, "Good grief, indeed."

Somehow, Rhonda managed to drag herself down to the kitchen. John was cooking breakfast. To Rhonda's surprise, Melanie was keeping John company. John was smiling up a storm. "You didn't?" Rhonda heard John say.

Melanie looked so pretty wearing a white sweater over a tan dress. Yes, her bangs were still a little on the dorky side, but that was okay. "I didn't have a choice. That dog already bit me in my butt," Melanie laughed—well, snorted. Rhonda cringed. "I ran into the hospital screaming that a rabid dog had bitten my butt off... You should have seen the looks I got."

"I bet," John chuckled. He spotted Rhonda. "Melanie was telling me how a dog bit her--"

"I heard," Rhonda quickly cut John off. She brushed at a blue blouse with tired hands and walked into the kitchen. "I wasn't expecting you so early, Melanie."

"I wanted to test your blood sugar before you ate or drank anything," Melanie explained. "I'm also going to call your doctor and make an appointment. The sooner we get some blood work done, the better."

"My, you are efficient."

"That's my job." Melanie pointed to a scale she had brought with her. "I need to get your weight, Rhonda."

"So early?"

Melanie nodded her head. She picked up the medical folder she had begun on Rhonda. "Everything before breakfast. That's the best way."

"Oh, okay." Rhonda walked across a lovely kitchen and stepped up on a floor scale that was actually pretty impressive.

"You're my height. Maybe an inch shorter--"

"5' 7."

"You're a little underweight. We can fix that, though." Melanie wrote in Rhonda's file as she talked. "Let's test your blood sugar. I have the machine on the kitchen counter."

Rhonda looked at John as he smiled. Melanie was a good nurse. Rhonda had found herself a solid piece of gold. "Alright, dear."

Melanie went to work. "Your numbers are healthy, Rhonda. Good job!"

"Can I have coffee now?" Rhonda asked.

"Sure thing." Melanie put Rhonda's file into a brown briefcase. "John, since I'm on nurse duty, mind if I give you a quick once-over? How are you feeling?"

"Oh no. You stay away from me, Ms. Melanie." John began waving his hands and then hurried to scoop a sea of scrambled eggs out of a large frying pan. "I ain't never seen a doctor and I don't take no medication. I ain't going to start now. No ma'am."

"You might as well give up now, dear," Rhonda told Melanie. "John is one of the most stubborn men you'll ever meet when it comes to seeing a doctor." Rhonda sat down at a glossy round kitchen table that screamed money.

Before Melanie could respond, Brent dragged himself into the kitchen. "Going out for a walk," he announced.

Rhonda studied her son. He was wearing a gray jogging suit and holding his walking cane. That was okay. Normal. Acceptable. What wasn't normal was the red sling backpack he had on. "What's in the backpack?"

"Water. Snacks. A first aid kit. The usual," Brent tried to sound casual. He glanced at Melanie. Wait a minute. Was she... pretty? Well, the woman's bangs were a bit nerdy. That was all. And maybe if she sported a stylish pair of eyeglasses instead of wearing a pair of old dinosaurs. His mind started to wander. A little lipstick here, some eyeliner there... do something with the bangs.

'Whoa there!' he mentally slammed on the brakes. 'What are you doing? This is Melanie we're talking about. The enemy! The one you're planning to frame for theft and get arrested. Remember?'

But try as he might, a tiny voice in his head whispered, 'You know, with a little effort, she could clean up nice...'

'Shut up, brain!' Brent grumbled to himself.

Rhonda was prepared for her son. "The guest house is off limits today. I've called an exterminator. I've had Melanie move all her stuff to the guest room upstairs."

"You did?" Brent asked before Melanie could speak.

Rhonda held up a quick hand. "I don't know how fleas got into the guest house. I don't want anyone going near there until the exterminator assures me every flea is dead. John had set the security alarm. He'll let the exterminator into the guest house when he arrives."

Melanie looked at Rhonda with confused eyes. What was she doing? Why was she telling Brent a bag of lies? Then she looked at Brent. She saw Brent grinding his teeth together. "Of course, mother. I understand."

"Well, you best go for that walk," John urged Brent.

"Huh?"

"Your walk." John pointed at the sling backpack Brent was wearing. "Best get on. Nice morning to take a walk. Just stay away from the guest house. That security alarm is mighty sensitive."

"Yeah...well, I might take my walk later. I haven't eaten breakfast yet." Brent threw a sour eye at Melanie. Rats. His plan was spoiled. Now what? "I'll take my breakfast in my room."

"I bet you will," John chuckled.

Brent made his way out of the kitchen and back upstairs. "Mind telling me what was that all about?" Melanie asked.

"You sure threw cold water on that sour turnip," John burst out laughing. He slapped his knee. "I wished I had a camera!"

"I wish I could laugh too, John," Rhonda said, her voice heavy with disappointment. "But what my son was planning to do... it breaks my heart. We raised him better than this."

"Am I missing something?" Melanie asked.

Rhonda let out a miserable sigh. "You better sit down, Melanie." Melanie did as asked. Rhonda sighed again. "I was up all night trying to think of a way to make you like my son... and vice-versa. I couldn't come up with a single plan. And, Melanie, to make matters far worse than they need to be, my son was planning to plant money in the guest house and then call the cops. He was going to claim you stole the money."

Melanie stared at Rhonda with shocked eyes. "Wow..." was all she could say.

"That boy just ain't no good," John insisted. He hurried to fix Rhonda a cup of coffee. "But the boy is your son and it's only fitting that you don't want to throw him into a pit. I just think you're fighting a losing battle is all, Rhonda."

"Is a mother supposed to leave her son to drown?" Rhonda asked. "I have enough of my own problems. I don't need to be fretting over my son all the time."

"Oh, now, Rhonda," John softened his voice, "you ain't die anytime soon. You're as fit as a fiddle. I tell you that all the time. You just think you're sick is all."

"I am sick, John," Rhonda insisted. She took a quick sip of coffee and winced. "Too strong."

"You're just being fussy. You need food." John set off to fix Rhonda and Melanie a plate of breakfast food. Afterward, he excused himself. "I best take that boy of yours his breakfast. If you hear someone screaming, that'll be me killing him."

Rhonda waited until John left before speaking. "I only want my son to know what love is. Is that so wrong?"

"No... but, Rhonda... me? With Brent?" Melanie gasped, her eyes wider than dinner plates. "Brent hates me. If I dropped dead, he would shoot anybody who tried to do CPR on me."

"Is it that obvious?" Rhonda groaned.

"Afraid so." Melanie glanced at her breakfast plate. The food looked amazing, like something from a fancy restaurant. But instead of digging in, she burst out laughing. Her eyes sparkled with amusement as she asked, "Wait, was Brent seriously going to try to frame me?"

"Yes, dear." Why was Melanie laughing? Rhonda expected the woman to be spitting bullets.

"That's a riot. Me. Melanie Jenkins. A thief," Melanie giggled. "I can't wait to tell Dad about this. He's going to laugh until Christmas."

Melanie snorted as she laughed, a sound that was more adorable than elegant. "I mean, sure, I've been arrested once before, but being framed for theft? I can't even figure out an old Nancy Drew mystery." Melanie snorted again.

"Dear, this isn't a laughing matter. My son is devious," Rhonda insisted.

"Oh, who cares," Melanie said, trying to catch her breath between giggles and snorts. "Rhonda, I'm your nurse. A wannabe prankster isn't going to scare me off."

She grinned, wiping a tear from her eye. "Now that I know I've got Kevin from 'Home Alone' out to get me, I'll watch my step. No worries, I'll make sure not to open doors with flamethrowers attached or walk under paint cans."

Rhonda was shocked at Melanie's attitude. "You're not going to quit?"

"Quit? Over this? Nah. This is the most fun I've had since... well, since I punched Brent in eighth grade," Melanie replied as she picked up a slice of avocado toast.

Melanie went quiet, like someone had hit her mute button. Her brain started connecting the dots, and boy, was the picture ugly. Brent wasn't just annoying; he was full-on supervillain material. Stealing money? That's not a prank; that's a one-way ticket to Jailville. Melanie realized she could have lost her nursing license. Her career would've gone poof. Everything she'd worked for, gone in a snap.

Suddenly, Melanie felt a fire in her chest. She was mad. No, scratch that. She was furious.

"Dear, are you okay?" Rhonda didn't like the look in Melanie's eyes.

Oh, Melanie wasn't alright. But she was going to be. "Rhonda, you're my patient and I've signed a contract that commits me to you for one solid year."

"Oh, I would never hold you accountable to that silly contract," Rhonda waves her hand dismissively.

"Maybe you should." A smile crept across Melanie's face, but it wasn't her usual sunny grin. Oh no, this was her "I've got a plan" face, the kind that would make even a cartoon villain nervous. Her brain was cooking up something extra spicy, and Brent was about to get a taste of his own medicine. Suddenly, being nice felt so last season.

"Maybe I don't want to let you throw our contract in the trash." Rhonda stared into Melanie's eyes. "But my son--"

"Oh, Rhonda," Melanie said, her voice sweeter than a candy store, "revenge is like dessert - best served cold and with extra toppings." She took a bite of toast, chewing like she was imagining it was Brent's ego. "By the time I'm done, your precious son will be singing 'Sorry' on repeat. Then you can have what's left of him." She grinned, looking more like a shark than a nurse. "I'm going to show Brent just who is really in charge."

"I don't think that's a good idea." Rhonda was startled at Melanie's sudden confession. Not good. Oh my. Not good. No way. The war drums were sounding! Take cover!

"Just leave it to me, Rhonda. I'm going to take Brent down a few notches. When I'm finished with him, he'll be begging for mercy." Melanie narrowed her eyes. "You know, at first, I thought this was just rich-boy pranks. But the more I chew on it, the more it tastes like trouble. Getting arrested? That's not a joke, I could have lost my nursing license. Being arrested is a very serious matter."

"Well, dear--" Rhonda's forehead creased with worry.

"Rhonda, what's good for the goose is good for the gander. Brent fired the first shot. Now please, let me show him who is the real boss. When I'm finished, he'll leave me alone," Melanie vowed, eyes glinting with challenge.

Rhonda began to speak and then just sighed. Melanie was a terrific nurse. She sure didn't want to lose Melanie. And who knows, she thought, maybe—somehow—a miracle would take place and love would somehow take root and blossom. Right? Oh, who was Rhonda kidding. Melanie and Brent were going to end up killing each other. "Dear, I'm turning a blind eye. That's all I can say at this point."

"Good." Melanie flashed a simple and satisfied smile. "Now, let's talk about how I'm going to start living here instead of in the guest house."

"What?"

"You did say the guest house is off limits, right?" Melanie's smile turned into a calculated grin.

"Well, yes. But..." Rhonda didn't have any room to maneuver. "John will show you your new bedroom."

"Perfect. Now, let's eat."

Oh, boy. Rhonda felt her stomach sink. Brent wasn't the type to take a jab on the chin and walk away. If Melanie wanted a war, he'd put on war paint and charge onto the battlefield. "Yes," Rhonda sighed, "we might as well eat in peace while we can."

After breakfast, Melanie slipped into the guest house while John kept Brent occupied. She filled a suitcase with some clothes, grabbed her toiletry bag, and sneaked back into the main house. After getting situated into a lush guest bedroom that was fit for a spoiled queen, Melanie hurried down to the main kitchen. "Did he see me go back to the guest house?"

"Nah. Kept that dummy on his bed while I pretended to look for a mouse. That boy screams like a woman when he sees a mouse." John folded his arms over a brown button up shirt and grinned. "Got the stuff?"

Melanie pulled a bottle of liquid laxative out from her dress pocket. "Let's do this."

"Girl, you've won over my heart right and left. I ain't ever gonna let you leave this place," John chuckled. He quickly filled a drinking glass with cold orange juice. Melanie added the liquid laxative—the entire bottle. "He won't taste it?"

"The laxative is tasteless," Melanie promised. He patted John on his shoulder. She was starting to feel very fond of John. "Okay, my partner in crime, take the inmate his medicine."

"You bet I will," John chuckled.

Melanie proudly folded her arms, looking proud, as John left the kitchen. "Brent will be on the toilet for the next three days. This is only stage one of my attack. By the time I'm finished with that jerk, he'll be begging for mercy," she said, her eyes twinkling with mischief.

John walked upstairs and knocked on Brent's bedroom door. "Come in! You better have a mouse trap, too!" an angry voice yelled.

John walked into Brent's room. Brent was still on his bed. "I called the exterminator. Just calm your britches," he spoke in a casual voice. "Drink this orange juice. When I was in Vietnam, we learned that rats don't like the smell of oranges. When we sweated, our sweat smelled like oranges. Kept the rats away."

Okay. Yeah. John's story was lamer than a duck that couldn't tell a funny joke. But, so what? John knew Brent didn't have enough smarts to kill a spider. Brent could sell stocks. Yes. The guy had a good mind with that kind of stuff. But everyday life? No way.

"Really?" Brent asked.

John handed Brent the glass of orange juice. "Yep. You just drink this glass of orange juice down while I go downstairs and find some mouse traps. Be back shortly."

As soon as John left, Brent chugged down his orange juice like a man dying of thirst. "Stupid mouse," he grumbled. "Bet Melanie smuggled it in under those crazy bangs of hers."

Brent put his glass down and flopped back on his bed, determined not to move until the exterminator arrived. "Now, how do I get rid of her?" he wondered, not realizing he was about to have much bigger problems.

Meanwhile, downstairs, Melanie was watching her watch like it was a ticking time bomb. "In about... oh... ten minutes, our resident grump will be doing the potty dance," she grinned. "And with that bum knee, it'll be more of a potty shuffle."

Right on cue, Brent's stomach started to feel funny and make a strange sound... and then... oh boy! The flood gates opened. Brent clutched his belly and cried out in agony.

Melanie and John high-fived, while Rhonda cringed in the parlor. There was nothing else the poor woman could do as her son hobbled to the bathroom taking miniature baby steps in order not to poop all over himself.

Brent made it halfway there before... well, let's just say the bedroom carpet would need replacing.

Revenge, as they say, is a dish best served... smelly.

Chapter 6

The Attacks Continue

B rent spent two full days sitting on a toilet feeling a bit confused. What had given him such bad diarrhea? Maybe the orange juice John had served him was bad? It never crossed Brent's mind that Melanie had sabotaged him. By the time Brent was able to stay away from the bathroom, Melanie had schemed up a new plan.

Meanwhile, Melanie's brain was cooking up more mischief. As soon as Brent could finally leave the bathroom without sprinting back, she put her next plan into action.

Melanie and John crept upstairs carrying a pet store box full of furry surprises. Brent was sleeping like a log. Snoring up a storm.

John tiptoed into Brent's room, quiet as a mouse... which was fitting, considering what he was about to unleash. He set the little white mice free on Brent's bed, grinning like the Cheshire Cat.

Back in the hallway, Melanie was holding in her giggles like they were hiccups. "Ready to make Brent the unwitting star of America's Funniest Home Videos?" she whispered, phone at the ready.

John's eyes twinkled with mischief. He was loving Melanie's pranks. "Let's give him a wake-up call he'll never forget," he chuckled.

John hurried back to Melanie. "Okay, get ready," he chuckled.

Melanie had her cell phone ready. "I'm ready to win ten thousand dollars for sending in the greatest funny video America will ever see."

"You bet." Boy, John was sure taking a liking to Melanie. The way a dad takes a liking to a lost daughter he never knew he had. "Let's do this."

"Go for it!" Melanie gave John a high five.

John sneaked back into Brent's bedroom. The white mice were scurrying about on the bed. John watched Brent roll over onto his left side. One of the white mice decided to get up close and personal with Brent's face. Unbelievable—and perfect! John drew in a deep breath and yelled; "Brent! Rats! Rats on your bed!"

Melanie had her phone ready, determined not to miss a second of this Oscar-worthy performance. And boy, did Brent deliver!

Melanie never saw a man jerk out of a deep sleep so fast. When Brent's eyes yanked open the first thing he saw was a white mouse smiling at him through a pair of cute little eyes. Brent let out a shriek that could have been heard in China. His entire body seemed to lift up off the bed as he shrieked.

"I'll get them!" John pretended to start swatting at the bed.

"Get them off! Get them off!" Brent rolled over to his right faster than lightning. Bam! He rolled right off the bed and hit the floor. "Get them off me!"

Rhonda came running down the hallway. She spotted Melanie aiming her cell phone into Brent's bedroom. "What in the world--"

Melanie silenced Rhonda with a quick finger and kept filming. Rhonda peeked into her son's bedroom. She spotted John pick up what appeared to be a white mouse. "Oh, these ain't rats. These are just some white mouse the exterminator left behind to catch that snake."

"Snake? What snake?" Brent hated snakes more than he hated vermin.

"Exterminator found a bed of snakes behind one of the walls. He managed to kill the snake eggs but the momma snake got away," John answered. He scooped up the white mice. "I best get these guys back downstairs. Reckon they got out somehow."

John hurried out into the hallway and closed the bedroom door. "Did you get it?" he asked Melanie.

"Sure did," Melanie snorted.

"Oh, you two..." Rhonda rolled her eyes. "First the laxative and now this. I should fire the both of you for tormenting my son." Rhonda had no venom in her voice. Just the opposite. She was actually amused. When Melanie said she was going to bring her son down a few notches, she meant it.

"Round three starts in a few minutes," Melanie promised and then dashed away like a girl running to a candy store. Rhonda moaned.

John chuckled. "The boy has what's coming to him."

Brent was too busy having a heart attack to hear Melanie's

getaway giggles. He crawled onto his knee like a wounded soldier, scanning the bed for any sign of the furry invaders. The mice had vanished faster than his dignity.

Just as Brent was about to let out a sigh of relief, his stomach gurgled. "Oh, no, not again," he groaned and then hobbled into his bathroom. Brent had nothing left to... uh... poop. His stomach was drained. He passed a lot of gas that smelled awful. "I'm going to sue whoever made that orange juice."

When Brent walked back into his bedroom, he heard someone knock on the bedroom door. "Come in, mother!" Brent assumed the visitor was his mother. Boy was he wrong.

Melanie waltzed in wearing a very old-fashioned nurse's uniform. The kind of uniform nurses wore in the 1920s. She even had the hat and shoes. "Rhonda asked me to check on your knee. John said you fell out of bed," Melanie spoke in a stern, cold voice. "I was also informed you've been having issues with your stomach."

Brent gaped at her, his brain trying to process what his eyes were seeing. "Going to a costume party?" he finally managed.

"Rhonda has asked me to dress in traditional attire. Now, please come sit on this chair and allow me to check your knee," Melanie commanded.

"No thanks." Brent hobbled back to his bed. He had landed on his bad knee pretty hard. "Tell John to bring me some Tylenol and orange juice... uh... coffee. No orange juice. Never again."

Melanie held back a grin. She was in character. "I have your mother's health to consider. If you have a stomach bug, I need to know." Melanie reached into a pocket. She pulled out a tongue depressor coat with ghost pepper paste John whipped up. "Please, allow me to look at your throat."

"My throat?" Brent croaked, instinctively protecting his face like she might punch him again.

"Yes, your throat." Melanie declared, marching over to Brent in a no-nonsense type manner. "Open your mouth. Let's see if your tonsils are as stubborn as you are."

Brent looked up at Melanie. A goofy woman dressed like a time relic was telling him to open his throat. But as Brent stared at Melanie's face—closer than usual—he noticed something: Melanie was actually very pretty. A little on the dorky side, sure. But very pretty—very, very pretty, in fact. Behind the large pair of dinosaur glasses the woman was wearing stood a beautiful pair of eyes that Brent had never noticed.

'No, no, no,' Brent's inner voice screamed. 'This is Melanie we're talking about! Enemy number one! The bane of your existence! The woman with surprisingly beautiful eyes...'

"Get away from me--" Brent started to say, his voice weaker than he'd like.

"Open your mouth!" Melanie ordered, her tone brooking no argument.

"Oh, alright," Brent mumbled, opening his mouth like a reluctant kid at the dentist. 'The sooner I do this, the sooner she'll leave,' he thought. 'Maybe I do have a stomach bug.'

As Melanie leaned in, Brent caught a whiff of her perfume. It smelled like roses after a summer rain, or like someone had bottled up a perfect spring day. 'Wait, when did Melanie start smelling so nice?' he wondered.

He tried to remind himself that this was Melanie. But his brain wasn't listening. It was too busy admiring how her eyes sparkled behind those ridiculous glasses.

'Stop it, Brent!' he scolded himself. 'You're supposed to be getting rid of her, not... whatever this is!' But even as he thought it, he couldn't help but notice how cute Melanie looked in that silly old-fashioned uniform.

"Open your mouth!" Melanie ordered in a stern tone. Brent did as told.

"This tongue depressor is coated with a medicine that might taste a little hot. Don't let it bother you." Melanie plastered the tongue depressor in her hand down onto Brent's tongue.

At first, all Brent felt was a tiny tingle. 'This isn't so bad,' he thought. Then the heat cranked up... then more... and more. Then whoa momma! Fire!

"Water!" Brent yelped, his eyes bulging.

Melanie took a step back. "I need to look at your throat--"

"Water! Fire! Help!" Brent crashed off the bed and began crawling toward an open bathroom door. "Water..."

Melanie grinned. "I told you the medicine was a little hot. Stop being a baby! Come back here!"

"Water. Water..." Brent begged, feeling like someone had poured gas in his mouth and lit a match. He couldn't think straight.

He crawled to his fancy bathtub, moving fast despite his hurt knee. Brent turned on the cold water and stuck his whole head under it.

Melanie walked into the bathroom just then. She saw Brent lying in the tub, cold water pouring over him. His hair was all wet, sticking to his face.

She snorted and burst into giggles. Brent looked silly, like a kid who'd eaten something way too spicy.

Melanie tiptoed out, grinning. Mission accomplished.

Brent didn't care that he was almost drowning himself. Brent dunked his face in and drank like he'd discovered water for the first time. His belly puffed up as he gulped the cold water.

He stumbled out of the tub, dripping everywhere and looking like a soggy puppy. "She did that on purpose!" he yelled, dripping on his designer bathroom rug.

Lave began to pour from Brent's eyes. He was sure now that Melanie had tricked him. Oh, Melanie was going to get it!

Brent managed to stand up and hobbled back to his bedroom. Melanie was waiting. "You did that on purpose! You tried to kill me!" he hollered at Melanie.

"Oh, poor baby!" Melanie made a clicking sound with her tongue. "Can't stand the heat?"

"You're fired!" Brent yelled.

"You can't fire me, Dumbo," Melanie grinned. Then she leaned back against the bedroom door and crossed her arms. "What? Can't handle it?"

"I'm calling the police!" Brent threatened, his voice ricocheting off the marble walls.

"Better tell the cops to arrest me for stealing money you planned to put into the guest house!" Melanie snapped. She stopped smiling. Her eyes became fierce. "That's right. I know what you were going to do!"

Brent froze. Uh oh. He was in trouble. What to do? What to do? Deny the truth. Yeah. That was the ticket. "You're crazy! Get out of here!"

"Your mother told me what you were planning, Brent. That's why she made up the story about the fleas!" Melanie eyed Brent with disgust. "I could have been arrested. I could have lost my nursing license. Do you know how hard I worked to become a nurse? How many hours I studied? No, you don't because you're a self-centered, egotistical, jerk!"

"Get out!" Brent yelled.

"Listen up. I'm staying in this house. Not the guest house. This big, beautiful house. For a whole year. You better get used to it. And if you ever, and I do mean ever, try to pull a stunt like the one you had in mind, I'll torture you so bad... oh, you won't know what hit you!"

As John stared at Melanie's angry face a few light bulbs began to go off in his head. "The orange juice. You drugged the orange juice. And the mice..." he said, realizing what had happened.

Melanie unfolded her arms. "Gee, I don't know who put a bottle of liquid laxative in your orange juice? Maybe we should call Sherlock Holmes and Watson?" she stated in a sweet and innocent voice.

"Good day to you." Melanie grinned and left the bedroom.

Brent plopped down onto the edge of his bed. He rubbed his

face. "That Amazonian snake drugged me."

Usually, Brent would have been steaming mad. Instead, something strange and alien happened. Brent's mind ran back through the years. He landed right in the middle of Mrs. Green's English class. He saw himself looking at a pretty girl who was reading a book. Her hand was on the pages.

"She's beautiful." Brent said quietly, surprised by his own thoughts.

Brent saw himself staring at a young Melanie for a long time. Then he heard an annoyed teacher clear her throat and ask Brent to focus on his work. Melanie looked up just in time to see Brent take his eyes off her. No one could know that Brent liked Melanie. All of his friends made fun of the dorky girl. He would be a laughing stock. Brent had to be cool. Only... deep down... he had it really bad.

"I didn't want to call her that mean name," Brent said to himself. "All of my friends were there watching me."

Pride? Yeah. Brent had pride. After Melanie socked him in the nose and humiliated him, he created a hard bitterness against the girl that covered his true feelings. Now, Brent was seeing the Melanie he had fallen in love with so many years before.

But he wasn't sure what to think. He used to believe women were deceptive creatures. Right? Yeah... but Melanie didn't come across as deceptive. In fact... well, Brent was actually impressed that Melanie had stood up for herself.

He touched his belly and then his tongue. "The liquid laxative was a nice touch," he thought, almost admiring her trick.

A curious grin touched Brent's eyes. Wow. He had really pushed Melanie's buttons. Melanie had pulled out a sharp set of claws and tore into him.

"She sure looked cute in that costume. Wait, what am I saying?" Brent shook his head. "That woman is a nuisance. I have to get rid of her." Only now Brent wasn't so sure if he wanted to get rid of Melanie. He grabbed his head.

"Don't be stupid! You're not falling for some dopey nurse. You're Brent Miltmore. You only date high class women. Women who attended Harvard and speak ten foreign languages. I bet Melanie can't even order a cheeseburger the right way."

Rhonda listened to her son mumbling to himself from the hallway. "It can't be, can it? Is my son falling for Melanie?" Hope erupted. Rhonda gasped. Could it be? She had never heard her son talking to himself in such a way. She had heard her own husband talking to himself in the same way before he proposed.

"Oh my," Rhonda said quietly.

The bedroom door burst open. Rhonda rushed in like a momma running to her bear cub. She grabbed Brent's hands before he could say a word. She looked into a pair of tormented eyes. "Oh my... it's true. You're falling for Melanie!" Rhonda squealed, sounding more excited than a kid on Christmas morning.

"What? Mother, are you drunk?" Brent tried to pull his hands away. Rhonda held on. "Mother--"

"You liked that girl in school. I remember," Rhonda said, her eyes sparkling like she'd just solved a big mystery. "I found papers with her name all over them. You wrote 'Melanie' more times than you've said 'No' to me in your entire life."

"Mother--" Brent tried to interrupt, his face getting redder by the second.

"Brent, please," Rhonda begged, her voice softer than Brent had heard in years. "Just be honest with me for once. Let your heart do the talking instead of your big, stubborn brain." She looked at him, hopeful as a kid asking for a puppy. "Do you like Melanie?"

Brent was about to say no, but then he saw a tear roll down Rhonda's face. "What do you want me to say?" he asked, his voice softer than usual.

"The truth," Rhonda pleaded. "The whole truth and nothing but the truth."

"Okay. Here's the truth!" Brent bowed his head. "Lara ripped my heart out. I thought I loved her. I wanted to love her..." Brent pulled away from Rhonda. He turned his back, as if he couldn't bear to face her.

"I swore I would never trust another woman ever again. When I remembered who Melanie was, all I could remember was how she humiliated me. But now..." He paused, sounding like the words were being pulled out of him. "I'm starting to see the girl I liked in school. Okay? Happy now? Satisfied? Great, now someone can just put me out of my misery!"

Rhonda's face brightened and she gently put her hands on Brent's shoulders. "I always knew you were hurting, honey. A mother always knows. I've been hoping for a miracle. I think maybe Melanie is that miracle."

"That crazy squirrel put liquid laxative in my orange juice--"

"I know. Isn't it wonderful?" Rhonda said, smiling.

Brent turned around. "Why would that be wonderful?"

"Because you've finally met a woman who is willing to stand up to you instead of chasing your money. You finally met a woman who has no interest in you. You're on the same playing field," Rhonda smiled. "And now, my son, it's up to you to be a man and win that woman's heart."

"Win her heart? Mother, you must be drunk!" Brent said, his eyes wide with disbelief.

Rhonda laughed, sounding happier than she had in years. "And you're in love!"

Brent groaned and slumped in defeat. "Go get a gun and shoot me now because... yes, mother... I think I might be falling in love with that crazy nut all over again"

Little did Brent know, Melanie was right outside in the hallway. She'd come upstairs to hand in her resignation- no salary was worth a year of Brent's attitude. But when she heard Brent's confession, her jaw dropped. She clapped both hands over her mouth, spun around, and raced downstairs, her undelivered "I quit" letter forgotten.

"John... oh my... John!" Melanie called out, sounding as excited as a kid on Christmas morning. "You're never going to believe what I just heard!"

Chapter 7

A Date?

Melanie didn't know what to think or do? She never gave Brent much thought. Especially not during her school years. Sure. She had caught Brent looking at her a few times but so what? Brent was always rude to her. Finally, Melanie had hit the end of her rope and punched the guy in his nose. Now, of all things, Brent had confessed to his mother that he... was... what? In love with Melanie? That's what it sure sounded like.

John could barely believe his ears. "You must have been hearing things," he insisted.

"I heard Brent loud and clear," Melanie said, pacing around the kitchen that John called his second home. "John, what am I going to do?"

Before John could say a word, Rhonda came hurrying into the kitchen. "You were out in the hallway, weren't you? I heard the floorboards creaking!"

"Yes, I was in the hallway," Melanie admitted, her voice soft. "I came upstairs to find you because I was planning to quit my job."

Rhonda ran to Melanie and grabbed her hands. "Oh please,

Melanie, give my son a chance. He's not a bad guy. He's been hurt. That's all. He closed himself off."

"That boy is full of pride and ego, Rhonda," John insisted, shaking his head.

"I know, John, but he's still my son." Rhonda looked into Melanie's eyes. "You do have such beautiful eyes. Don't let those eyes become filled with bitterness and regret."

"Rhonda--"

"Melanie, you became a nurse because you care about people. Well, my son is carrying a sick heart that needs healing," Rhonda insisted. "Give him a chance. That's all I'm asking."

"What are you proposing?" John asked in a troubled voice. "I've taken a liking to this girl, Rhonda. I don't want to see her get hurt."

"One date. Here at the house. A dinner date. Tonight," Rhonda answered in a hopeful voice.

Melanie's pretty face twisted into knots. What was she supposed to say or do? "I need to go call my Dad. Excuse me," she said, her voice shaky.

Melanie rushed outside into a cold wind and with trembling fingers, she called her Dad.

"Dad, I'm in trouble!" she blurted out as soon as he answered. "Help!"

"Calm down. Calm down. Tell me what's wrong?" Howard asked.

Melanie blurted out the entire scene in one long breath. "Dad, I punched Brent in the nose when I was in school with him for crying out loud! Now he thinks he's in love with me!"

"And you really put liquid laxative into his orange juice?" Howard asked in amazement.

"Yeah, and that's not all," Melanie said, her voice getting higher. "I posted him screaming like a girl over some mice on the internet a couple of hours ago," Melanie winced. "So far the video has gotten over five thousand views."

"Ouch," Howard said. "Sounds like you've been busy."

"What should I do, Dad?" Melanie's voice wobbled like she was about to cry. "Should I pack my bags and run for the hills?"

"Not on your life!" Howard said loudly. "You're a Jenkins! We do not retreat from a battle. You stand your ground and stand firm doing it! If you don't like Brent Miltmore, you tell him to leave you alone or I'll come over there and tear his back side off with my bare hands. If you like Brent Miltmore... well, maybe have dinner with the guy. Who knows? Maybe I might get a grandchild before I'm too old to remember my name."

"Dad!" Melanie squeaked, her face turning red. "A grandchild? Really?"

"Well, I'm not getting any younger here, Melanie," Howard complained. "Brent comes from a good family. You could do a lot worse. Besides, the guy is loaded. I wouldn't have to worry about you having a good retirement."

"Dad, I don't care about money--" Melanie started.

"I know, I know," Howard cut in. "But it doesn't hurt. Look, all I'm saying is give the guy a chance. If he survives your pranks and still likes you, he might be a keeper. Or just really, really stubborn."

Howard paused, then added, "Listen, sugar pie, just do what

feels right. You're thirty-five now. You're old enough to decide things for yourself. And hey, if it doesn't work out, you can always prank him again."

"Dad!" Melanie laughed.

"Now, I gotta go. The sports section is calling my name. Bye now!"

"Dad... wait..." Melanie said, but her dad had already hung up. She lowered her phone and stared at it like it might give her the answers. What was she going to do?

Then, like a lightbulb turning on, a thought hit her. What was she getting all worked up about? So what if Brent suddenly liked her? It's not like she had to marry the guy tomorrow.

"Get a grip, Melanie," she told herself. "You're acting like you're back in high school." She took a deep breath, trying to calm down.

"Okay, here's the plan," she said to no one in particular. "I'll just tell Brent, 'Thanks, but no thanks,' as nicely as I can. Then I'll focus on taking care of Rhonda. That's why I'm here, after all." Melanie drew in a deep breath, shaky breath and tried to settle her nerves.

She nodded to herself, feeling a bit better. "Yes. I can do this. I'm a professional nurse, not a teenager with a crush. I've dealt with worse things than a guy who likes me. Like that time Mrs. Johnson tried to escape the hospital in her bathrobe."

The only problem was Melanie wasn't sure how to feel? She stood there, feeling more confused. One minute, Brent tried to frame her for a crime she didn't commit. The next, the guy was confessing his love for her? No way. "Life doesn't work out that way," she muttered. "Maybe Brent has a mental disorder?"

She paced back and forth, her mind racing. "Is he crazy? Did a mouse build a nest in his brain while he was sleeping?" Something. Melanie didn't know. She shook her head, trying to make sense of it all.

Then she stopped, hands on her hips. "Why am I freaking out? I've dealt with crazies in the past before. A good can of bear spray and a swift kick to the manhood area always worked." She could take care of herself.

"But was Brent really a threat?" she wondered out loud. "Or just confused?"

Melanie let out a big sigh. "Good grief."

Melanie looked at the house and took a deep breath. "Time to face the music," she muttered, and walked back inside.

Rhonda pounced on her the second she walked in. "Well?" she asked, her voice full of hope.

"Rhonda," Melanie started, trying to keep her voice steady, "your son was going to have me arrested. I can't just forget that--"

"Oh, let's just forget about that little misunderstanding," Rhonda interrupted, waving her hand.

She grabbed Melanie's hands, grinning from ear to ear. "We'll start fresh. Clean slate. How about a nice dinner? John can cook something fancy for you two. It'll be like one of those TV dating shows, but with less drama. Well, maybe."

Melanie blinked, feeling stunned. "Dinner? Rhonda, I don't think--"

"Great!" Rhonda cut in, not waiting for an answer. "I'll tell John to get cooking. Nothing says 'forgive me' like his famous truffle mushroom risotto, right?"

"And I'll pay you one hundred thousand dollars!"

John's jaw nearly hit the floor. "Rhonda, are you nuts?"

"No," Rhonda said, her eyes suddenly fierce. "I want my son to find love! Melanie, if I have to bribe you to have dinner with my son so you can see the real him, then that's what I'll do!" She squeezed Melanie's hands. "There's a good man hiding inside my son. He just needs the right woman to bring him out."

Melanie saw the sad desperation in Rhonda's eyes. How could she say no?

"You don't have to bribe me," she said softly. "I'll do it. But just this once. I've got nothing to lose except maybe my appetite. Besides, you're my patient, and I don't want you getting so worked up you actually get sick."

"Splendid!" Rhonda beamed and hugged Melanie. "Oh, thank you, dear! You won't regret it."

"John, grab the car keys. We're going to Pierre's Market - we need their finest truffles and that incredible aged risotto rice!" Rhonda said, practically bouncing with excitement.

John could only shake his head, looking at Melanie with sympathy. "I hope you know what you're getting into."

"Me, too," Melanie whimpered.

Before anyone could say another word, Rhonda grabbed John's hand and zoomed out of the kitchen.

Melanie stayed in the kitchen for a while. She was afraid to leave. "What if I run into Brent?" she thought, her heart doing little jumps.

Then, the worst possible thing happened. Brent limped into the kitchen with his cane. "Oh," he said, looking surprised. "I thought the house was empty."

"Uh, Rhonda and John just left for that fancy market downtown. They're getting... um... something special for dinner." Melanie tried to sound casual.

Good grief. She was alone in a giant house with a man who could be crazy. Only Brent didn't look crazy. Instead, Brent looked, well, tired. Just tired. No fight was in his eyes.

"Mother told you about dinner, huh?" Brent asked. Melanie nodded, not trusting her voice. "Mother didn't give me much of a choice to say no. She started to cry and everything. I can never say no to my mother when she cries."

Brent added, "It's her secret weapon. Works every time."

"So..." Melanie said, searching for words. "I guess we're having dinner."

"Guess so," Brent agreed. "Should be interesting. At least the food will be good."

"Yeah," Melanie said. "And hey, if it gets awkward, we can always talk about how you tried to get me arrested."

Brent winced. "About that..."

"Save it for dinner," Melanie said quickly. "I have a feeling we'll need conversation topics."

She took a deep breath. "Brent, I heard you and Rhonda talking upstairs. I heard what you said." Melanie tensed up even more. "I think it's sweet that you think you have feelings for me and all but let's face it. I'm not exactly your type." Melanie decided to get the issue out into the open and throw cold water on the fire before the fire could spread.

"You're telling me," Brent said, surprising her. He hobbled to the kitchen table and sat down like an old man settling in for story time. "Did you know I had a crush on you in school?"

Melanie's eyebrows shot up so high they nearly left her face. "What?"

"Yep. But I couldn't admit it. Had to act cool for my friends. They thought you were a nerd." He shook his head. "And when you broke my nose? Boy, did I hate you for humiliating me. My friends ragged me to the end of the earth and back. They never let me live that moment down."

"Well," Melanie said, trying not to smile, "you did call me a 'stupid moose' if I remember correctly. Not exactly a great pickup line."

"You remember correctly," Brent confirmed. He was too old to act like a silly grade school boy.

"Melanie, I'm sorry I came across so harshly. I'm sorry I wanted to get you arrested. My pride was wounded and the sight of you just reminded me of all my past failures." Brent said, his voice softer than before.

"You could have made me lose my nursing license." Melanie said, still upset.

"I didn't think about that. I'm sorry. No more tricks. I promise." Brent looked up at Melanie. He thought she looked cute. Really cute. But not just cute... beautiful even. "You are very beautiful. So was Lara."

"Lara?" Melanie asked, confused.

"A woman I wanted to marry." Brent lowered his eyes. "Lara ripped my heart out. After that I swore I would never trust a woman again. When you showed up, I remembered how embarrassed I felt when you hit me. A lot of sore feelings erupted inside of me. It seems like every woman I try to give my heart to ends up making me bleed." Brent sighed. "I have a problem with my ego and pride. When I get hurt, I lash out. I don't mean to. I just do."

Melanie listened, surprised by Brent's honesty. Was Melanie seeing the real Brent Miltmore? She didn't know what to say. This wasn't the Brent she expected.

"Well, at least you're confessing the truth now." Melanie sat down across from Brent. She looked into his face for a long minute. Really looked. Instead of seeing a bitter, self-centered jerk, she saw a handsome man who didn't know how to process his feelings. A man who was knotted up on the inside.

"When you grow up rich, a lot is expected of you. You have to hang out with the right group of people. You have to make the right grades. Wear the right clothes. Talk the right way. There was no way I could let anyone know I had a crush on you. I didn't mean to call you the name I did. You're not a stupid moose."

"I accept your apology," Melanie said. "Just don't try to have me arrested again."

"Deal," Brent promised. "No more medicine in my orange juice?"

Melanie smiled. "I can't promise that." Brent frowned. "Just kidding. Deal."

Brent smiled. A real smile. Not a fake smile. And Melanie's smile was real too. And pretty. And welcoming.

"Are we still on for dinner tonight?" Brent asked.

"Why not? If we back out now, Rhonda might never forgive us," Melanie said.

She thought about it. Did Melanie really want to have dinner with Brent? Suddenly, she found herself actually considering spending the evening with Brent. Brent was kind of cute. Maybe once he lightened up, he might be a little fun to hang out with. But what about love? Oh boy. Melanie pushed that notion out of her head quicker than a mouse going after cheese. The thought of falling in love with Brent scared her.

Brent nodded. "My mother means well. After tonight, I'll tell her we just aren't compatible."

"Yeah," Melanie agreed, but she wasn't sure if she meant it. Was Brent and Melanie compatible? Melanie had no idea? She didn't even know Brent very well.

"Uh, mind if I look at your knee? You wobbled in here like it was hurting," Melanie asked, switching into nursing mode.

"You don't have to—" Brent replied.

"There might be some swelling." Melanie insisted. She asked Brent to show her his knee. He hesitated, then agreed. Melanie checked his knee gently. "Your knee is really swollen. We need to put some ice on it."

Brent watched as Melanie got to work. Melanie retrieved an ice pack from the freezer. She put the ice pack on Brent's knee and then fetched him two Tylenol.

"You are a good nurse. Very caring." Brent said, sounding surprised.

Melanie thanked Brent for the compliment. "Thanks. I just really like people. I think we're meant to enjoy being around each other. I know there are some rotten apples out there. Maybe even more rotten apples than good ones but it's the good apples that make it all worth it."

Brent looked thoughtful. "Most people don't see it that way. I sure don't. I see people as a threat. It feels safer to keep everyone at arm's length."

"That sounds lonely," Melanie said softly.

Brent nodded. "It is. But it's also safe."

"If you live your life that way, how will you ever find love?" Melanie challenged.

"Have you ever found love the way you live your life?" Brent countered.

"I... well..." Melanie stammered, hating how easily he'd found her weak spot. "Let's just say that the right man has never crossed my path."

"You lived in Los Angeles. Los Angeles is a very populated city full of people. I seriously doubt the right man never crossed your path."

Melanie winced. Brent was pushing her into a corner. "I... well, it's complicated."

Brent heard something in Melanie's voice he had heard in his own voice millions of times. "You're afraid of love. I get it."

"No... it's just that..." Melanie could no longer defend her position. She sat back down. "Okay, maybe a little. I mean, why shouldn't I be? The thought of getting married terrifies the poop out of me. I dream about getting married all the time but to take the plunge? I get cold chills. And to have a baby? I've delivered babies before. I've seen the pain, mister... oh boy, have I seen the pain! P-A-I-N!"

Brent grinned. Melanie was silly. Dorky. But funny. No woman had ever made Brent smile like this before. Melanie had a good sense of humor. An eccentric one, but good.

"Well, if it helps," Brent said, "the thought of changing diapers scares the... poop... out of me too, so to speak. I wouldn't know what to do with a crying baby if you paid me all the money in the world."

"Forget changing a diaper," Melanie said. "How about childbirth? I saw a woman in labor so long I thought my hair would turn gray. Ever hear a woman scream so loud the doctors run away in fear?"

"No," Brent said, looking both amused and a little scared.

"Let me tell you. Childbirth is no picnic. You're pushing a watermelon through a tiny little grape." Melanie grimaced in pain. "And some women have several babies! I have nightmares at the thought of giving birth to one baby."

Brent laughed. "You paint quite a picture."

"I aim to terrify," Melanie said, grinning. "But seriously, it's scary stuff. Beautiful, but scary."

Why was Melanie confessing her fears to Brent? She wasn't sure.

But strangely, it felt nice just sitting and talking with Brent instead of being enemies.

"Maybe you could adopt," Brent suggested.

"I'm not the soccer mom type," Melanie said.

"Oh, I don't know? You might make a good mother," Brent objected. "You're a very caring person."

"How about you? Ever think of becoming a dad?" Melanie asked.

"No... no...and no!" Brent began waving his hands into the air. "I'm a self-centered jerk who only cares about his yacht and Lamborghini, remember?"

Before Melanie could control her mouth, she blurted out: "It seems to me that you're just lonely."

"Ditto for you," Brent fired back, but not in a mean way. In fact, his voice was soft and caring, which surprised even him.

Melanie stared into Brent's eyes. Brent held her look. Was something happening between them? Was romance blossoming? Melanie had no idea. She felt her heart leap as she stared into Brent's eyes. How could she fall in love with a guy who'd schemed to destroy her?

Somewhere deep inside Melanie's sacred heart, she heard a voice whisper: You're about to find out.

Chapter 8

Love

Melanie stepped into the dining room, her heart racing. She felt like a completely different person, and it wasn't just the clothes. Rhonda had insisted on the lovely blue evening gown that fit like a dream, styled her bangs perfectly, and somehow even convinced her to swap her thick, Coke-bottle glasses for contacts. The unfamiliar sensation of eyeliner and the soft scent of perfume made her feel... elegant. It was strange, but in a way that made her stand a little taller, walk with a touch more confidence.

She caught her reflection in the polished glass doors and almost didn't recognize herself. This wasn't the usual Melanie—the one who spent most of her days in scrubs, hair up in a messy ponytail, often avoiding her own reflection. She'd always been comfortable as the dorky one, but for tonight, just this once, she allowed herself to be something different. And it felt... nice.

Rhonda admired Melanie with a motherly pride. She had been the one pushing for this transformation, but even she hadn't expected it to work this well.

When Brent saw her, he nearly choked on his water, completely caught off guard. His usual smirk vanished, replaced by wide eyes and stunned silence. This wasn't the Melanie he was used to. No, this was someone else entirely.

His brain struggled to catch up. The Melanie he knew was a little awkward, but now? She was breathtaking. The elegant gown, the way her bangs framed her face, the soft glow of makeup—it all hit him like a punch to the gut. He'd never seen her like this, and for a moment, he couldn't quite believe it was the same woman.

Melanie's eyes landed on Brent, and for a second, she almost didn't recognize him. He was dressed in a sharp suit—one that, by the looks of it, probably cost more than she made in a year. His hair was neatly slicked back, a subtle hint of cologne blending with the delicate aroma of the dinner, and for the first time, she had to admit... he looked really handsome. There was an unexpected softness in his expression, something almost endearing beneath his usually polished exterior.

Brent shifted awkwardly, smoothing the front of his jacket as if he wasn't quite used to the formality himself. There was a nervous energy around him, something Melanie wasn't used to seeing. Brent was always so sure of himself, always so quick with a snarky comment. But now, standing there, he seemed a little out of his depth—vulnerable, even.

He cleared his throat and looked at her, his eyes lingering a little longer than usual. "You look... amazing," he said, his voice soft but sincere, as if he was surprised by his own words.

"Thank you," Melanie replied softly, feeling a bit silly. Her gaze shifted to the dining table, eyes widening. "Wow, look at the table." Romantic candles casting a soft, warm glow over an array of delicious-looking dishes. It was perfect.

Just then, John entered the room with a gentle smile. He gave Melanie a nod of approval, clearly pleased with her transformation. "Your seat, ma'am," he said warmly, pulling out a chair for her.

Melanie couldn't help but smile back at him. "Thank you, John. Everything looks amazing."

John gave a humble nod before turning his attention to Brent. "Enjoy the evening," he added with a wink, before slipping back into the kitchen.

"Since I'm on pain meds," Brent said with a sheepish grin, "I asked John to swap the wine for sparkling cider. Hope that's alright?"

Melanie's smile widened in relief. "That's more than alright. I don't drink either. Looks like we're the life of the party tonight."

But even with that small connection, she couldn't shake her nerves. Why was she so jittery? She'd worked in the trauma department, for crying out loud—seen mangled bodies, chaotic emergencies. And yet here she was, fidgeting with her hands in a lovely dining room, anxious just having a conversation with Brent.

"I'm sure dinner will be excellent," she said, her voice slightly too high, betraying her nerves.

"Yeah, yeah... sure," Brent agreed, nodding a bit too eagerly. If Melanie was nervous, Brent was worse. His usually calm, cocky demeanor was nowhere to be found tonight.

And then, as if the universe had decided to have a laugh, disaster struck.

Brent reached for his glass of sparkling cider with a little too much enthusiasm. His hand darting out too quickly and—yep—the wine glass went flying. Sparkling cider splattered everywhere, but most of it landed right on Melanie's dress.

"Oh no, I'm so sorry!" Brent stammered, shooting up from his chair to fix the mess. But in his rush, his knee buckled. Before he could even register what was happening, he stumbled, crashing to the floor with a thud. As he went down, he yanked the entire tablecloth with him.

Plates, bowls and glasses began crashing down, clattering onto Brent in a symphony of chaos.

"Brent!" Melanie shouted, jumping up from her chair and hurrying around the table. She had barely reached him when her feet slipped on a puddle of spilled soup. Before she knew it, her legs flew out from under her, and she came crashing down... right on top of poor Brent.

Brent groaned, grabbing his ribs. "Ow!" he cried, wincing in pain.

Panicking, Melanie scrambled off him, eyes wide as she noticed Brent clutching his side. She wanted to apologize a thousand times, to fix everything—but then she saw it. His face, smeared with soup and dripping with cider. The sight was so ridiculous, so completely absurd, that instead of crying, she burst into laughter.

It started as a soft giggle, but within seconds, she was laughing uncontrollably. And then, of course, came the snorting. "Oh my, Brent," she gasped between fits of laughter, "Your face. Your *face*!"

John and Rhonda rushed into the dining room, eyes wide at the scene. Melanie was kneeling beside Brent on the floor, surrounded by spilled soup, overturned plates, and a wine glass rolling off the table. John just sighed, rolling his eyes as he turned to leave.

Before Rhonda could even open her mouth to react, John gently grabbed her hand and pulled her with him. "Let 'em be. Let love be love, Rhonda," he said with a soft smile, leading her out before she could start crying over the mess.

Meanwhile, Brent laid on the floor, covered in soup and cider, utterly embarrassed. He could feel the sticky mess dripping down his face and saw Melanie still laughing, her dorky snorts breaking through her giggles.

"I... oh, forget it," Brent muttered, shaking his head in defeat. "Who am I kidding? I was never meant to find love anyway." He started to push himself up, feeling the sting of embarrassment more than anything else. He didn't want to be the punchline to some joke—not tonight.

"Oh, don't be sore. I'm not laughing *at* you. I'm laughing at us, Brent. Just look at us," Melanie snorted. "Our first date and I've got soup all over the backside of my dress. And you're covered in soup." Melanie continued to laugh and snort. "If this isn't one for the record books, I don't know what is? If I was writing a book, I wouldn't know how to end our story?"

Brent quickly realized that Melanie laughing at the chaos around them. And honestly, he had to admit, the situation was pretty funny. Silly, yes. Disastrous, absolutely. But funny. And in a weird way, maybe even a little romantic.

Before he could second-guess himself, Brent reached up and gently brushed a strand of hair away from Melanie's eyes. Something shifted between them, and without thinking, he pulled her down softly, their lips meeting in a quiet, unexpected kiss.

Fireworks? Oh boy. You know it. Brent melted into Melanie's kiss like butter on a hot stove. And Melanie? She felt herself melting too, just as sweet and warm as jelly being spread out on toast. Or at least, that's how she would describe it later to Rhonda.

Rhonda, of course, had no idea what Melanie meant by that. Melanie always had the strangest ways of explaining things. But what mattered were the fireworks! Boom! Bang! Explode! It was everything Melanie had secretly hoped for. And more.

When they finally pulled away, both of them were breathless and a little dazed, staring at each other with the kind of shared wonder that only happens in moments like these.

"Why... why did you kiss me?" Melanie whispered, her breath shaky, her face still inches from Brent's. Her heart was racing, and she needed an answer.

"I've always wanted to kiss you," Brent whispered back, his voice soft but steady. His eyes searched hers, as if trying to understand what had just happened. "Why did you let me kiss you?"

"I... I don't know," Melanie stammered, her voice barely above a breath. Then, without thinking, she grabbed Brent's face and kissed him again—this time with passion and certainty, a kiss that would go down in the books. When she finally pulled back, she gasped, her eyes wide. "Wow!"

"Wow is right." Brent muttered, still struggling to catch his breath. But before he could fully recover, he pulled her close again, kissing her in a way that sent her heart spiraling. His kiss was deeper, more intense, and it knocked the air right out of her.

Melanie's knees gave out, and she collapsed right on top of him, both of them laughing between breaths, the world around them forgotten.

"See," John said quietly to Rhonda, standing just outside the dining room door. "You've just got to let them be and let God do what He does best."

"Guide the hearts," Rhonda sighed, a soft smile tugging at her lips. She gave John's hand a gentle squeeze before slipping back into the kitchen, leaving the new couple to their moment.

Brent held Melanie in his arms, not caring about the mess around them. Melanie rested her head on Brent's chest, listening to his heartbeat. "Funny," she said.

"What?" Brent asked. He felt happier than he'd ever been, even while sitting in a puddle of soup and cider.

"I never thought love was like this. I always thought it had to be perfect."

"Me too," Brent agreed.

Melanie giggled. "You're cute when you're covered in soup."

"So are you," Brent said, pulling her closer. "So, what now?" he asked.

"I don't know," Melanie admitted. "I guess I'll need to wash the soup out of my hair."

"I mean... what about us?" Brent asked, his voice serious. "Melanie, I don't want to get hurt again."

Melanie looked up at him, her eyes soft. "I don't want to hurt you, Brent. And I don't want to get hurt either. But I think I want to try. With you."

Brent's face lit up. "Really? Even after everything?"

Melanie rolled over and looked into Brent's eyes. She could see he was being completely honest. "Does this help?" she asked, leaning down to kiss him.

"What does that mean?" Brent asked, his voice hopeful and a little scared.

"It means I'm never going to hurt you," Melanie promised.

Then she took a deep breath. "But Brent, this isn't really me. This dress, these contacts. I want you to love me for who I am. I like my glasses and my normal clothes. I wanted to look beautiful tonight, but I want you to love the real me."

Brent reached up and touched her face gently. "Melanie, whoever you are... I love. I fell for you long ago. You weren't wearing a fancy dress and contacts when we were in school."

Melanie smiled, her eyes getting a little watery. "You mean you'll still like me in my dorky glasses and comfy sweaters?"

"Yes," Brent said. "Glasses, sweaters, and all."

"Good," Melanie said, "because I think I like you too. Grumpy attitude and all."

Brent touched Melanie's face the way he would touch a soft rose petal. "What is your favorite color? I've always wanted to know."

"Yellow." Melanie said, smiling.

"What is your favorite book?" Brent asked.

"'Halos' by Kristen Heitzman."

Brent's mouth dropped open. "I've read that book!"

"Really?" Melanie looked surprised.

"Yes," Brent insisted. "Alessi Moore, right? She had her Mustang stolen?"

"'Yes. I love Alessi!" Melanie exclaimed. "When did you read it?"

"A few weeks ago, actually. I can't remember where it came from. I just found it in my bedroom. I was bored. So, I started reading it." Brent looked at Melanie and then laughed. "Could this be our 'Halos'?" he asked.

"Yes. Yes. Yes!" Melanie squeezed Brent excitedly. Brent winced in pain. "Oh, your ribs. Sorry."

What happened next was so strange that Melanie and Brent would have trouble explaining it later.

Out of nowhere, a small yellow butterfly appeared. It gently landed right on the tip of Melanie's nose. Melanie went cross-eyed trying to look at it.

"Don't move," Brent whispered, his eyes wide.

The butterfly sat there, its wings slowly opening and closing. Then, to their amazement, it flew down and landed on Brent's nose.

Melanie watched, her mouth open in shock. "Are you seeing this?" she whispered.

Brent nodded slightly, afraid to scare the butterfly away.

After a few seconds, the butterfly took off again. It flew up and away, disappearing as quickly as it had come.

Melanie and Brent looked at each other, both stunned.

"Where did that butterfly come from?" Brent asked. He was confused. He'd never had a butterfly land on him before, let alone on his nose. And it was autumn - butterflies usually only came out in warm weather. Plus, it was yellow, just like Melanie's favorite color.

Melanie looked at Brent with big, surprised eyes. Was this a sign that Brent was meant to be her husband? "I have no idea," she said softly. She put her head back on Brent's chest.

Brent didn't know what to say. Where did that butterfly come from? He didn't tell Melanie - not yet - that on the night his father proposed to his mother, a yellow butterfly had appeared out of nowhere.

Melanie didn't tell Brent - not yet - that when a kind old woman died under her care at the hospital, a yellow butterfly had suddenly appeared in the room.

They both lay there, thinking about the strange butterfly and what it might mean. Neither of them spoke about it, but both felt like something special had just happened.

"That was weird, huh?" Brent finally said.

"Yeah," Melanie agreed. "But nice weird."

"Nice weird," Brent repeated, smiling.

They fell quiet again, just enjoying being close to each other, both wondering what surprises life might bring next.

Chapter 9

A Splash of Romance

The next day, Melanie walked beside a picturesque lake, colorful leaves crunching beneath her feet. A cool breeze blew as she wrapped her arms tighter around her warm brown coat. Her glasses were back on and her dorky bangs were back in place.

As she stared at the rippling water, her thoughts drifted to Brent. Did she really love him? What about that mysterious yellow butterfly? Why had she kissed him—and more importantly, why had she kissed him back?

"It felt so nice to be kissed," Melanie whispered to herself, a goofy smile creeping onto her face. She could still feel the warmth of Brent's lips, and for a moment, she let herself bask in the memory. But then... reality hit.

"Today's a new day. What if Brent's changed his mind?"

After all, he had been on heavy painkillers last night, loopy from his bum knee and practically drowning in medication. What if that clouded his judgment? What if that sweet confession of love—and the kiss—were just the result of too many painkillers?

"Oh no," she muttered, stopping in her tracks by the lake's edge. She pressed her hands to her forehead, staring down at her reflection in the water. Did he even know what he was saying? What if I was just... a side effect?

She let out a sigh. "Great. I'm the girl who gets kissed because of pharmaceuticals. That's just... awesome."

The truth was, Brent wasn't exactly known for heartfelt declarations. Snark? Absolutely. Charm? On occasion. But emotional vulnerability? Not a chance.

What if he completely regrets it? What if, at dinner tonight, he looks her dead in the eye, and says, 'Yeah, so, about last night—let's just pretend that never happened.'

Melanie groaned, imagining the awkwardness. She had dealt with all kinds of disasters working in the ER, but this? This was a whole new level of emotional trauma. And what was she supposed to do—ask him? What if he replied, "Well, you're nice, but I was also on painkillers, so..."

Ouch.

Knowing her luck, Brent was probably already rethinking his life choices at this very moment.

Suddenly, the unmistakable sound of hoofbeats interrupted her spiral of doubt. Melanie looked up, eyes widening in shock—and then pure delight.

There was Brent, galloping towards her on a majestic horse, wearing... was that a Cupid costume? Complete with wings and a tiny bow and arrow? He looked utterly ridiculous and completely adorable.

Instead of laughing, Melanie found herself tearing up. Brent pulled the horse to a stop in front of her, grinning from ear to ear.

Brent rode up to Melanie. He carefully dismounted, favoring his good knee as he lowered himself down.

"Melanie Jenkins," he said, his voice full of emotion, "you're worth looking foolish for. You're worth tossing my ego and pride in the trash. You're worth everything."

Melanie's heart skipped a beat as Brent reached into his costume and pulled out a small white box. He opened it, revealing a stunning diamond ring that sparkled in the autumn sunlight.

"When I was a boy," Brent continued, his eyes never leaving Melanie's, "I always dreamed about marrying you. I didn't care where you lived or how much money you had. None of that stuff mattered. You mattered. I was a fool then, and I don't want to be a fool anymore."

Tears were now running down Brent's face, matching the ones forming in Melanie's eyes. "Will you do me the honor of completing my every dream by becoming my wife?"

Melanie felt her heart swell with love. This man, who she'd once punched in the nose, who'd tried to frame her, who'd driven her crazy, was now kneeling before her, offering his heart.

"Yes!" Melanie cried, throwing herself into Brent's arms. "Yes, I'll marry you!"

Well, that would have been a perfect fairy tale ending, except...

When Melanie ran into Brent's arms, she knocked him off balance. Brent stumbled backward toward the lake, his Cupid wings flapping uselessly. He grabbed Melanie's hand, trying to steady himself, but it was no use. With a spectacular splash, they both tumbled into the chilly lake water.

Brent came up first, sputtering and spitting out water. His Cupid costume was plastered to him, and his fake wings drooped sadly. "The ring!" he gasped, patting his pockets frantically.

Just then, Melanie surfaced, snorting up a storm. "Looking for this?" she asked, holding up the slightly damp ring box.

Brent's eyes widened in relief, then narrowed playfully. "You saved the ring but not your fiancé?"

"What can I say?" Melanie grinned. "I have my priorities."

They looked at each other, soaking wet and ridiculous, and burst out laughing. Brent's Cupid costume was ruined, Melanie's glasses were askew, and they were both shivering in the autumn air.

"So," Brent said, pushing his wet hair out of his eyes, "still want to marry me?"

Melanie pretended to think about it. "Well, I suppose so. After all, how many women can say their fiancé proposed dressed as a waterlogged Cupid?"

Laughing, they collapsed into each other's arms, right there in the lake. As they kissed, a familiar yellow butterfly fluttered by, as if to say, "Well, that's one way to start a life together!"

Meanwhile, from a discreet distance, John lowered his binoculars and rolled his eyes. "I can't imagine what kind of kids those two will create. Have mercy."

Rhonda, standing beside him, just smiled. Her eyes twinkled with mischief and joy. "You know, John, for once I don't feel sick anymore. In fact," she said, straightening up with newfound energy, "I feel well enough to plan a beautiful wedding!"

John groaned good-naturedly. "Oh no. Here we go again."

"Come on, John," Rhonda said, grabbing his arm excitedly. "We've got work to do."

As they walked back to the house, John shook his head fondly. "Well, at least life around here will never be boring."

"Boring?" Rhonda laughed. "With those two? John, my dear, we're just getting started!"

And as if to punctuate her words, they heard a distant splash and laughter from the lake. John and Rhonda looked at each other and burst out laughing.

⸎⸎♡ ♡♡ ♡⸎⸎

"Brent is getting married?" Logan Hunnicut asked, his voice full of disbelief. "Aunt Rhonda, we're talking about my cousin, right? Mr. High and Mighty Brent?"

"That's right," Rhonda assured Logan. "And Brent wants you to be his best man. Probably because he doesn't have anyone else. You're my last hope. So, please say yes."

"Well, Aunt Rhonda, I live in Oregon. Vermont is a long way off and I don't fly--"

"Please, Logan. I'll pay for everything. Five-star hotels, the works," Rhonda begged, pulling out all the stops. "You and Brent were once such close friends. He's changed, I promise. You'll see."

Logan looked into a bathroom mirror as he talked on the phone, running a hand over his stubbled chin. He needed to shave. What for? No reason. Logan worked as a freelance writer. His office was his den. Logan could walk around all day wearing a turtle costume and no one would care.

Not that he would. Logan might not be big on ego or pride, but he did consider himself a handsome fella. "Well," he muttered to his reflection, "I guess we'll see how I stack up next to the great Brent Miltmore."

"The wedding is in two weeks, Logan," Rhonda's voice crackled through the phone. "Please. I've never asked you for a favor but might I remind you I did help you buy your house."

Logan could practically hear Rhonda's guilty wince. She hated twisting his arm, but desperate times called for desperate measures.

"I remember. I remember," Logan sighed, bowing his head in defeat. "Alright, Aunt Rhonda. You win. I'll come to the wedding. I'll be Brent's best man. I promise."

"Good," Rhonda beamed, her voice dripping with satisfaction. "I knew you'd see it my way. Oh, by the way, I need you to do me one tiny favor."

Logan's smile faded. "Aunt Rhonda..."

Melanie has a cousin who lives in Salt Lake City. Lacey Liu is her name. Lacey is afraid to fly, just like you. She is also afraid to drive a car or take a train or a bus. She has this phobia--"

"Aunt Rhonda--" Logan groaned again.

"Logan, I promise Melanie I would ask you to pick Lacey up. Now I can't disappoint my future daughter-in-law, can I? For

crying out loud. I'm not asking you to pick up a herd of bulls."
Rhonda wouldn't be deterred.

Logan sighed deeply. "Okay, okay. Calm down. I'll pick up this
Lacey Liu woman. But Aunt Rhonda, it's going to be a long road
trip. You know how particular I am about my truck."

Rhonda rolled her eyes. And she thought her son was a
headache. "I know, Logan. Just make sure to be in Salt Lake City
in two days. Now, get a pencil and write down Lacey's address."

Logan did as Rhonda ordered. He scribbled down an address
and then ended the call.

"If that woman wasn't family..." He shook his head, then read
the name aloud. "Lacey Liu, huh?" He paused, tapping the pen
against the pad. Maybe I should give her a call to let her know I'm
coming."

But as he glanced at the address again, a small smirk tugged at
his lips. He had no idea what he was in for.

꒰꒰꒰♡ ♡♡ ♡꒱꒱꒱

Meanwhile, in Salt Lake City, Lacey Liu was frantically tearing
apart her living room trying to find her inhaler.

"Travel... I can do this," she wheezed, her voice a mix of
determination and impending panic attack. "I love Melanie. She's
my cousin, after all. I haven't seen her in years, but blood is thicker
than water... and possibly as thick as my anxiety right now."

Lacey fumbled through a messy desk drawer. "Where is my
inhaler?"

If Logan had been in Lacey's home, he would have been in for quite a shock. He would have seen a woman in farm overalls and mismatched socks, racing around her small living room like a panicked chicken. Her hair stuck out in all directions, as if she'd just been electrified. She moved with the energy of someone who'd had way too much coffee, her eyes wide and wild. This chaos would have been enough to make him wonder if the road trip was a bad idea. And that was before he even met the cat.

To say Lacey was a little on the crazy side was being kind. Lacey Liu was to paranoia what Mozart was to music - a virtuoso. She was so paranoid she jumped at her own shadow.

Beautiful? Undeniably. A gifted writer? Award-winning. Crazy? Oh yes.

Her latest bestseller, "50 Shades of Anxiety: A Love Story," had critics raving and therapists booking extra sessions.

"Bobtail, where is my inhaler?" Lacey whined.

A mean-looking cat, who enjoyed terrorizing rabid raccoons for fun, stared at her unblinkingly. This was not your average cat. No, Bobtail was what you'd get if you crossed a honey badger with a wolverine and sprinkled in a dash of Hannibal Lecter for good measure.

Bobtail adored Lacey but hated everyone else. And where Lacey went, Bobtail followed. Bobtail was her emotional support animal, after all.

Little did Logan know, he was in for the trip of his life—one that would lead him straight to the woman he'd been waiting for. And all he had to do was survive a cross-country road trip with a beautiful, neurotic woman and her demon cat.

Oh, and did we mention Logan hated cats? And that his miniature pinscher, Rocky, shared his feline aversion with a passion?

As Logan picked up the phone to call Lacey, the universe chuckled. This was going to be one heck of a ride.

Dear Reader,

Thank you for spending time with Brent and Melanie as they discovered that sometimes love starts with a punch to the nose. If you enjoyed their story of pranks and romance, It would mean the world to me if you'd consider leaving a review here on Amazon .

Coming soon in Book 2 of *The Matchmaker* series:
When Brent's cousin Logan (a procrastinating writer with an overprotective dog) gets stuck driving Melanie's cousin Lacey (and her demon cat) across the country to the wedding, Aunt Rhonda's matchmaking radar starts pinging. The next installment of this series promises more chaos, romance, and proof that Aunt Rhonda's schemes always lead to love—even if the road gets a little bumpy.

With gratitude and love,

P.S. Yes, Rhonda's already plotting Book 3!

Create Review

☆☆☆
☆☆☆

www.ingramcontent.com/pod-product-compliance
Lightning Source LLC
LaVergne TN
LVHW020240240625
814536LV00009B/486